423385882\6919428

PS
3616
.E84277
S86
2009

DISCARDED

MN

Summer Mirage

Sub-Title:

Death of a Hired Man

Carrol P. Peterson

authorHOUSE

OCT 1 2 2009

NORMANDALE COMMUNITY COLLEGE
LIBRARY
9700 FRANCE AVENUE SOUTH
BLOOMINGTON, MN 55431-4399

AuthorHouse™
1663 Liberty Drive, Suite 200
Bloomington, IN 47403
www.authorhouse.com
Phone: 1-800-839-8640

This is a fictional story and any resemblance of characters found here which may resemble persons, living or dead, is purely coincidental and not intended.

© 2009 Carrol P. Peterson. All rights reserved.

No part of this book may be reproduced, stored in a retrieval system, or transmitted by any means without the written permission of the author.

First published by AuthorHouse 2/2/2009

ISBN: 978-1-4389-4136-3 (e)
ISBN: 978-1-4389-4134-9 (sc)

Library of Congress Control Number: 2008911533

Printed in the United States of America
Bloomington, Indiana

This book is printed on acid-free paper.

Foreword and Dedication

This book is meant for mature readers. This novel is a "slice of life" and contains a lot of realism and naturalism. Some finicky readers who have been used to reading stories, like "Little Women" or "Alice in Wonderland," might object to the profanity in this novel. I grew up on a Minnesota farm and know its lifestyle. A person hears profanity or corrupted English on farms, in factories and in the military...sometimes even in offices.

Like most writers, I drew from both my experience and education in writing this book. I started on it while residing in Tucson, Arizona during 1971 and completed it while living at Long Beach and the Bakersfield, California area that same year. SUMMER MIRAGE is the first novel I have written.

I dedicate this book to the American farmers who work hard from sunrise to sunset, they who curse a little after being kicked by a dairy cow, for they are the necessary people who feed the rest of us in the towns and cities. For my part, I came close to remaining on my home farm, or in the military, if the situation had been right. I enjoyed both those lifestyles.

July 31, 1983 AD

Mr. Carrol P. Peterson

The Rude Farmer

I had left Minnesota with my car loaded and an itch to travel. I parked my 1952 Chevrolet in the farmyard owned by a farmer named Clifford. It was good farmland in northern Illinois and the terrain was level.

That day, Cliff and I stood there in the hayloft doorway, him talking and blowing farts at the same time."One good thing is that you are older than you are," he stated.

Did he mean that I was well-matured for my age? I wondered.

By sunset, Cliff strolled in the yard, with shirt off and drinking wine.

That night, in the milking parlor, I milked many a dirty cow on that hot summer day. Cliff was age 40, and I age 20, while I espied another hired man, Ben, dark-haired and strange, carrying a hay bale.

"The daughter stopped her car by that cornfield," I said, while pointing.

"She probably stopped to take a leak," replied Ben.

The teen-aged girl later fried eggs for Ben and I. When she had walked out, Ben spoke, "Her dad will be wondering where the hell she has been."

I drove the hard-steering Model A John Deere the next day, raking hay. Then it was my turn stacking hay bales in barn.

After tiring, I said, "I'm not going to stack another bale. I come here to milk cows." That was a tough day."I'll milk those shittin' cows any way you want tonight," I continued.

Cliff, infuriated, grabbed me by the shirt. "Do you think you can come on a place and tell them what to do?" he questioned.

Hours later, I overheard Cliff telling his wife, "One man is through."

"Which one?" she asked.

"Pete, the dairyman is leaving."

The fair-haired lady pondered a moment. "I liked him," she replied.

The rude farmer paid me off then, in July of 1959, $8.00 for two days work. While driving out of the yard, I heard him say to me, "Wait a minute." I kept on going, for distrusting that World War II veteran of the European theater, I considered him a jerk.

Carrol P. Peterson

December 1, 1981

Chapter One

The rare summer fog was lifting as the sunbeams filtered through the oak and elm trees bordering the green fields. The sturdy teenager, Chester, on his family farm in southeastern Minnesota, was mending a barbed wire fence. With a hammer and a pocket full of staples, he was walking near the row of wooden posts when he sighted a red fox squirrel climb a dead tree and hide in the hole at the top.

He found a long stick in the pasture and after some effort, reached the top of the dead tree. While he was poking the stick in, the squirrel escaped from a side hole. The stick hit metal.

Chester finished the fence mending; and when he reached the wood frame, red machine shed, his dog Adolf, a black and white English shepherd, rushed towards him.

He petted the dog and said, "I will grab an ax and chop down the tree." He said this as if Adolf could understand his thoughts. His mother Lucy, brown-haired and slim, emerged from the long, low, red chicken coop with a pail of white eggs.

"What are you up to today?" queried Lucy.

"I aim to check out a dead tree," replied her son.

"There are only bugs in that," retorted Lucy.

Chester was soon chopping at the tree. "This is tough work, Adolf," he said as his dog looked on. One more swing and it toppled over.

After a while, he had the metal box free. With curiosity mounting and with eager, summer-tanned hands, the brown-haired youth opened the cover.

"Holy smokes! There are some gold coins and a yellowed roll of paper here!" stated Chester. He carefully picked up the paper and read it:

"Our gang from Missouri failed in the robbery of the First National Bank in Northfield, on Sept. 7, 1876. Mr. Miller and a couple of others were killed. Cole Younger was wounded and captured and may be at the Stillwater prison by now. On the way north, we robbed a bank president on a road near Mason City and took $7,500 in twenty-dollar gold coins. There are five coins in the box here. The rest are in another steel box hid in a cave one mile east of Fremont, Minnesota. Jesse and I hid the money in fear of being captured. We are escaping back to our homes and will return in a later year when things look safe.

Frank James Sept. 14, 1876

"This is a great mystery and opportunity for me!" said Chester to his trusty dog. He made up his mind to only tell his best friend, Rusty Wampuch, a farm neighbor.

Before long, he espied Rusty on his bicycle as he emerged over the gravel road, and they waved to each other.

"I was coming to see you today," said the red-headed youth.

"Something big has come up!" replied Chester.

His younger friend parked his green and white bike by an elm tree and faced his handsome neighbor.

Chester gazed up at the big, white cumulus clouds and hesitated to find the words. "Do you remember the Jesse James' raid on the bank at Northfield about seventy-five years ago?"

"Yeah, only what I heard in my history class. The tough Norwegians fought back and killed three crooks, but Frank and Jesse escaped to the forest," replied Rusty.

"Look what I found this afternoon while mending fences," said the other. Chester proudly displayed the rusty box with the gold coins and weathered paper.

Rusty took his time reading the hand-written paper.

"You are right, Chester; this is something big!" he said with sparkling eyes. Rusty pondered a moment and added, "We should not tell anybody, not even my brother Sam. Leave out your brother Louie and our parents too," he continued.

"That seventy-five hundred dollars in twenty-dollar gold coins might even be worth more money today," said Chester.

"Tomorrow let's ride our horses to the Fremont store and ask Frank if there is a cave nearby," Rusty suggested.

Chester took hold of the yellowed paper and turned it over. "There is more writing on the back! The metal box is buried under an Indian painting on the cave wall!" he said excitedly.

Rusty also examined the paper.

The following morning, Chester was up and about just after the roosters did their daily crowing. He helped milk the twenty Holstein cows and rinsed the Surge buckets after letting the cows out to pasture. His dad, Ole, with his beer belly or middle-aged bulge, watched his son saddle his golden palomino, Fury.

"Where are you going horseback riding?" Ole asked.

"Rusty and I are riding to the Fremont store," Chester responded.

"Don't stay too long because we got chores to do after five o'clock," retorted the farm owner.

"We might do some exploring, but we'll return to help with chores," replied Chester.

At that moment, Rusty, coming at a slow gallop, appeared on his bay horse, Tony. He reined in his mount as Chester put his foot in a stirrup and swung up into the saddle.

"Easy, Fury," he said.

"Hello, Ole!" shouted Rusty to the farmer watching from a barn door.

Ole waved his hand. The two pals were soon off in a cloud of dust down the dirt road.

"Let's race to the Fremont store!" shouted Chester.

"Good!" replied the redhead with freckles on his face.

Each slapped his speedy mount with the leather reins.

"Come on!" yelled Rusty to his quarter horse.
"Make dust!" hollered Chester to Fury.
They galloped past an August field of tall corn and a patch of clover and timothy. Two farm brothers were in the field with a John Deere tractor, and they were mowing down the hay. They waved at one another. A red fox ran across the gravel road and raced for the hardwood forest.

The riders turned a corner and soon pulled up at the old general store. An old man sat on a rocking chair. Rusty and Chester tied their horses to the iron railing.

"Howdy, Frank!" offered Chester while removing his hat.
"Hello, boys!" answered the store owner.
"Is there a cave in this neighborhood?" queried Rusty.
"I figured everybody knows about the cave one mile east on the Woodward farm. It's big enough on the inside to turn around with a load of hay," stated Frank. "Ride east one mile and then go north at the four corners."
"We will each buy an ice cream bar," said Rusty.

Frank got up slowly, letting loose two loud book-slamming farts and went into his wood frame store that was a century old. The boys each gave a nickel for the food and soon were in their saddles.

When they entered the Woodward farm, the owner greeted the two youths. "What brings you boys here?" he asked.

"Do you have a cave on your spread?" asked Chester.
"Oh, hell yes, it is over there by that grove of trees," the farmer replied while pointing.

"Is it okay if we check it out?" queried Rusty.
"Go ahead, but be careful at the entrance because it's kinda steep," replied Woodward. He opened the wooden gate and let the riders through the pasture to the cave.

The boys tethered their mounts to tree branches next to the cave. Rusty tied a rope to a tree, and both boys lowered themselves into the cave opening. They each carried a flashlight. They walked inside to espy a high ceiling and wide walls with some bats hanging from above.

"Look at the carvings on the wall and the old dates! I am also looking for the Indian paintings," added Rusty.

"There it is, dark forms on the wall!" said Chester.

The latter took out a small spade from his belt and dug into the sandy floor. Rusty discovered the bones of a calf that had fallen into the cave and died.

"That unlucky creature," he said.

The other dug for a half hour hoping to find a treasure.

"Give me the shovel and let me dig for a while," said his pal.

Chester handed over the tool. Meanwhile, the latter went to explore more of the cave and found an old rusty tricycle. Rusty also played out and gave up. They took turns digging and found nothing after two hours. The boys used their flashlights to examine the walls.

"Look, there are more paintings on the opposite wall!" said Rusty as he moved closer.

"I am not digging anymore today because we have to get home for the farm work," said Chester.

"I just thought of something. What if we find the treasure and old man Woodward claims it because it's on his land?" asked Rusty.

Chester scratched his head. "We will have to sneak it out and keep quiet or claim we found it on one of our farms and divide the money," concluded Chester.

They then climbed back to the top and mounted their horses to return home.

Some time later, Chester and his younger brother Louie, who also had brown hair and was a little on the heavy side, were busy carrying pails of ground oats and corn for the ducks on a pond.

"Did you see anything interesting in that cave?" Louie asked.

"Only some wall paintings and animal bones," replied Chester.

Meanwhile, on a nearby farm, Rusty and his younger brother Sam were feeding the chickens corn and oats.

"Where did you go riding with Chester today?" asked the other redhead.

"We went to the Fremont store; old Frank still charges a nickel for ice cream bars and candy, but bottled soda pop costs a dime," replied Rusty.

"No, shit!" returned Sam as he emptied a pail of feed for the Plymouth barred-rock chickens. The hens were hungry.

Some forty miles to the east in Wisconsin, another farm family was living out their drama of life, east of the great Mississippi River. It was said that people were a little different in another state. Certainly Bernie Baker was different.

One day Bernie was on the road to La Crosse. The city lay in a valley with wooded bluffs nearby. Oak, elm, and other hardwood trees were seen on the hills. The stars were shining on a summer night as a green car drove up a street. Bernie, about thirty-five years old with brown hair and an average build, parked his car in front of a tavern. He walked in and sat down on a stool at the bar.

A Seeberg jukebox was playing the number one tune, "Until I Waltz Again With You," by Teresa Brewer, the Bronx beauty. Bernie noticed a newspaper with the headlines, "Peace Talks Continue with North Korea."

"What will you have?" asked Sabrina, the cute, slim girl with blonde hair who was tending bar. She moved closer to him.

"Give me a bottle of Hamm's beer," replied Bernie.

A deer head was mounted on the wall, and from the ceiling hung old guns, knives, and wagon parts. Bernie ordered another beer. A baseball game between the Brooklyn Dodgers and New York Giants on the black and white television set gathered interest from the drinkers. A young couple sat next to Bernie.

"Where the hell did you pick up that whore?" he asked the young man.

Tom, wearing a brown suit, gave a cold stare. "Do I have to take that?" he asked the bartender.

"No, sir, you don't," replied Sabrina.

Tom then gave Bernie a hard right with his fist, and he toppled over chairs and a table. Tom was caught off guard when Bernie got up and slugged him in the mid section and then landed a fist on his kisser.

A fat cop arrived to break up the ruckus. The human bull dragged both men off to jail.

"You dumb shits have had enough for tonight," said the cop.

"Look, it was not my fault; that dumb farmer insulted my wife!" Tom said angrily.

"You were fighting," retorted the policeman.

"Any good man would fight in this case," returned Tom.

"Let me out of this puke hole!" shouted Bernie.

"You will never get out!" sneered the blue uniformed cop.

"Don't let the dude get near me, or I'll take care of him," said Bernie.

"You don't scare me," jeered Tom.

"You drunks can sleep it off tonight," said the cop.

Tom's wife, who had been watching, queried, "When will you let them out?"

"Maybe when the war is over."

Julia, the fair-haired wife, made a frown and stepped out the door.

The next morning, the officer opened the cell door.

"It's about time," said Bernie.

"Be out of town by sundown," growled the fat cop.

"Go to 'billy hell," said Bernie under his breath as he strolled outside. He was thinking out loud. "Let's see, it's Sunday early, and the saloons are closed."

Bernie walked into a church and knelt before sitting down. The black-robed priest was talking. Bernie whispered to a man next to him, "What the hell is he mumbling about?"

It was a beautiful church with thick wooden beams across the ceiling, and a green carpet was lying down the aisle.

When the service was over, Bernie walked out talking. "What the hell, let the old man do the work in the barn today. Why should I go home and clean out that stinking cow barn?"

He entered the Hollywood theater to see the movie, "From Here to Eternity". He bought a coke and popcorn and took a seat.

After the show, he entered a restaurant to order northern pike, apple pie, ice cream, and coffee. He lit up an Old Gold cigarette. A short time later, Bernie entered a saloon. La Crosse was full of saloons. He ordered a Rob Roy and soon espied a familiar face.

"Is that you, Marigold?"

A honey-blonde young lady turned her attractive form. "Hello, Bernie, what brought you to town?"

"I went to church and then took in a movie," he replied.

"Was it "From Here to Eternity", with those two skinny weaklings Frank Sinatra and Monty Clift?"

They sat in silence for a while as the Wurlitzer jukebox played "Your Cheating Heart," sung by Joanie James.

"Why did you come into this bar alone?" asked Bernie.

"I did not come alone; my friend Sally is nearby, and here she comes now. The latter was a good-looking brunette.

"Now isn't that a pretty sight; when are you two getting married in church?" she asked.

"Don't get funny, you teaser," replied Marigold. "We are going to the movies to see "Pickup on South Street", starring Richard Widmark and Jean Peters."

"I enjoy that kind of mystery," said Sally.

"I like westerns best," said Marigold.

"I'd like to make hay with Jean Peters," commented Bernie.

After the movie, Sally said, "Go with Bernie; I can drive home myself." She looked good in a yellow dress.

"Okay, if you say so," replied Marigold. "Good night," she added.

The couple climbed into the green car, and they left the city lights for the country.

"Are we going to park for a while?" she asked.

"No, I'm too tired," replied Bernie.

"You can take me home then," the blonde beauty said.

The car meandered down the long, lonely gravel road.

Chapter Two

They entered the driveway, and she stepped out of the car. "See you," the golden-haired damsel remarked.

"So long, sport," replied Bernie, and the gravel flew from the road as he took off.

A couple of miles more and he turned into his own farm road. On his folks' farm there was a windbreak of pine trees on the northwest side. When on the grass, Bernie looked up at the stars and saw the Big Dipper and Jupiter. Neptune, the black and white English shepherd, walked over to Bernie. He shook hands with his dog.

The next morning, Bernie pulled on his bib overalls and strolled towards the barn. The barred-rock and Rhode Island red hens were out making music as they walked around looking for something to eat. The barn was big and red, with brown wooden shingles on its roof. The granary, shop, corn crib, garage, machine shed, two brooder houses for chicks, and chicken coop were also red, while the Victorian-style frame house was painted white. There was a fifty-foot silo made of concrete next to the barn. There were oak, maple, walnut, cedar, and pine trees around the house and barn. Flowers were in bloom on that August day when Bernie entered the barn door.

Ben, his father, was milking a herd of cows using three Surge units. The usual farm smell was obvious.

"Christ almighty, what happened to you yesterday? You should have been here to help with the chores," said Ben, a gray-headed fellow.

"I wanted a day off so I jerked my green jalopy towards La Crosse," replied his son.

"Well, take over now; I'm heading for the house for breakfast."

Bernie took out the sponge from a small pail and wiped off the udders of more cows. Then he opened the barn door and let out ten cows. Several made a mess on the floor so he grabbed a scraper to push down the manure. Bernie took off a Surge unit and emptied it into a bucket before placing it on the next cow. A cow kicked him on his leg. He grabbed her tail and twisted it.

"You fuckin' son-of-a-bitch!" he yelled. Then he kicked the Holstein in the middle, and she heaved and pooped out a wad of green manure.

Bernie carried in another ten-gallon can from the milk house. The strainer pad was plugged up with dirt and flies, so he changed a pad and threw the dirty one on the floor. A yellow cat chewed on it. Another pad was hanging out of the cat's ass, and he pulled it out.

"That dumb cat!" said Bernie. The farmer finished milking and turned the cows out to pasture and scraped the cow shit into the gutter. He swept the concrete floor and spread lime over it.

Anna, his mother, had ham and eggs with toast on the stove when Bernie came in for breakfast. Ben was seated at the table.

"I suppose you were out girling last night."

"What does that mean?" asked Bernie.

"Chasing women," replied his dad.

"Every man who is now married was once a girl chaser," Anna spoke up. "That is how they get married because a man chases a girl until she catches him. Is not that how we got together?" She looked towards Ben.

"I suppose so," he replied.

"I put a new sickle into the mower, and you can start to cut the clover and timothy," said Ben.

"Okay," muttered his son.

Anna kept a neat kitchen; two calendars were on the walls.

"I wonder if Ike will end the Korean War this year?" wondered Ben.

"Maybe I should join up," said Bernie.

"You are too old," replied his dad.

"If I'm old, then you are ancient!" Bernie walked to the red gas barrel and turned the handle to put fuel in the green Oliver tractor. Then he grabbed the grease gun from the shop and lubricated the tractor and mower. Soon he was driving up a lane where he dismounted to open a one-wire electric fence.

He was now past the barnyard and out into the hayfield. He lowered the sickle and stripped the gears as he shifted them, like a man in a hurry. Bernie drove close to the fence in third gear. A woodchuck darted along the ground. Gee, this baby runs like a car! he said to himself. He looked back to see the mower plugged up and a long line of hay still standing behind the mower.

"Mother fuck, it's plugged up tighter than a baby's pink ass!" he snarled. He dismounted to pull out the green hay from around the sickle and bar. He then drove the tractor in a circle and came back in the same direction.

When he reached the end of the row, Bernie became aware of a horrible smell. He left the tractor, crawled over a fence, and walked to a ravine to search for the source of the rotten smell. There lay a dead cow, its body filled with white maggots and yellow worms.

He ran up the hill and back to the farmstead. Grabbing a five-gallon gas pail, he returned to the ravine. He poured the gasoline on the carcass and heaved a lighted match on it. Like a flash, there was a large blaze. It was the cow that had died last winter in the barn. She had been in a steel stanchion next to a hay chute which was not closed all the way during a winter cold spell and had caught pneumonia and died. She had needed to be pulled out with a rope hooked onto a tractor, Bernie remembered.

He sauntered back to the tractor and continued mowing hay. There were pocket gopher mounds that occasionally plugged up the mower. Bernie jerked out a cigarette and lit it using the exhaust pipe on the tractor. Later, while mowing, he heard a strange noise behind him. Upon looking back, he espied a yellow cat on the clover with two legs cut off.

"God dam cat, now I will have to go home and get my gun," said the farmer.

When he rounded the corner of the building, he halted the Oliver and went to the garage for the squirrel gun, a .22 rifle. On the way back, he shot a sparrow out of a tree and picked it up to heave it into the barn for the cats to eat. Those cats are crazy for birds, Bernie thought.

He soon was next to the injured cat; he shot it and then carried the dead animal to the barnyard and tossed it in the John Deere manure spreader. There were also a few dead chickens in the spreader waiting to be hauled out with the other crap.

That night, they had pancakes and lefsa for supper. Lefsa, a Norwegian food, was good with butter and brown sugar and when eaten while warm. Later, Bernie took the gallon pail to the barn to take off milk for the house. He wanted to take off from the best cow in the barn to use for the family's drinking and cooking needs. Later, Anna would strain it with a white sheet and then pasteurize it.

Ben was gone to town, so Bernie started to milk the cows. He carried out several ten-gallon aluminum cans, the strainer, the pail and sponge to wipe off the cows' teats, and three milking machines.

He went to the feed room to fill the cart with ground oats and corn with a shovel and then gave each stall a shovel of feed. There were forty stanchions in the barn all with oval drinking cups. Bernie opened the barn door.

"God damn it, where are those shittin' cows?" he yelled. He then mounted the Farmall "H" red tractor and rode out to look for them.

The herd was way down in the south forty acres. He chased them while riding on his rubber tire farm vehicle. His dog, Neptune, was handy in helping bring the cows home. Bernie stripped the gears as he shifted into high gear. He drove like a bat out of hell shouting, "Come on, you stupid bitches, get moving!" He almost ran into the hind legs of a cow fast on the run. They ran along the cow path, and the dust was flying.

The tractor wheels hit cow pies, and the shit flew into Bernie's face. He swore until he was red in the face. "I will have to take a bath tonight," he uttered.

Once the cows were all in the yard, Bernie shut the gate and chased them into the red barn. Some heifers were wary and hesitant about entering, so he picked up a stone and threw it at a shy one. That encouraged her to enter the large doorway. Most of the cows were in stanchions, but some had to be chased about. Bernie picked up a rubber hose and ran after the stubborn ones to whip them.

Soon, using brute force, he had all the cows locked up. He hung on a Surge bucket, but the cow behind him gave him three quick kicks in his back. He was knocked into the gutter that was full of cow manure and maggots. The farmer was a total mess.

Bernie grabbed a pitchfork and stuck the cow in her side. It bellowed in pain with blood running down its side while hot cow shit ran down the face of Bernie. Suddenly, Ben entered the barn.

"What in the holy shits is going on here?"

"That damn cow kicked me in the back."

"If you cut her stomach with the fork, she might die," said Ben in a concerned tone of voice.

Father and son then did the milking together. Later, Bernie went to the house for a bath.

"It looks like you fell in the gutter," said Anna.

"Yeah, and I also got kicked."

Then the trio watched Ford Theater on television, with an introduction by the handsome young actor, Ronald Reagan. Later, the farm family hit the sack for a good night's sleep.

Moonlight filtered into the windows as Ben and Anna Baker planned on attending a relative's funeral, and Bernie dreamed of meeting his pretty neighbor after the sunrise. Frogs were heard croaking in the pond, and an owl hooted in an oak tree. The house was not close to a township gravel road.

The next day, while his folks attended a funeral, Bernie made a phone call to Marigold, and she soon arrived on a bicycle.

"Hi, Bernie," she said while walking up the lawn, smiling.

"Hello, Marigold, come on in," he replied while opening the screen door in front. He took two bottles of Royal Crown Cola from the cooler, and they sat at the kitchen table.

"What is new?" queried the honey blonde.

"My folks went to Aunt Hilda's funeral; she finally kicked the bucket. You met her at a family picnic in the Community Park in Lanesboro," explained Bernie.

"Yeah, you played softball that day, and you pitched a good game," she replied.

"I remember. Let's watch some television," he suggested.

They sat down on a sofa, and Bernie had his arm around her. Matinee Theater was on the dark brown Philco model, and the show was in black and white.

As the drama ended, Bernie said, "I am going into the bathroom to shave."

Marigold came along and grabbed a Kleenex to blow her nose. She tossed it into the toilet and flushed it.

"I turn my back and look what she does," exclaimed Bernie.

They both laughed.

Soon they were strolling hand in hand among the farm buildings; they passed a granary and came upon a straw pile.

"Let's sit down on the straw since there is shade on this side," he suggested. The straw on top was rotten from the rain and snow of the past year.

"Did I ever tell you the story of Jack and Jill?"

"I never heard it yet," she replied.

"They were in a straw pile like this when it started to rain. There was a dugout where straw had been taken out with a pitchfork. So, Jack and Jill went into the dugout and stayed all night. During the happy hours, he lost his condom or rubber."

"What happened next?" queried his friend anxiously.

"Well, nine months later Jill had a baby, and he was born with a smile on his face and with a straw hat, wearing rubber pants."

"Oh, you devil," said Marigold with a smile on her pretty face.

Bernie laughed until his sides almost burst. The couple stayed in the coolness of the straw pile for a while.

"I have to be getting home," stated Marigold.

"Some drinks are in order first," he suggested.

Back at the house she gathered ice cream with honey for the topping. Bernie poured a glass of Bub's beer, brewed at Winona, Minnesota, and added a scoop of ice cream.

"This looks good," he added.

"Well, a beer float," said Marigold.

"It is the best treat under the sun," he replied.

She took a spoonful for a sample. "Delicious," was her reply.

They listened to Guy Mitchell sing "My Truly, Truly Fair" on a radio.

"I will see you this weekend," she added while rising from her chair.

"You bet," her pal said.

"Hey, where did you learn that 'you bet' figure of speech?"

"It originated with the Mississippi riverboat gamblers in the 1840s," responded Bernie.

"Well, you are not such a dumb farmer after all," she said with a laugh. Marigold then departed for her home.

A couple of days later, Bernie went out with the green Oliver tractor to rake up a field of clover and timothy. He saw a few black crows flying around, and a fat, red squirrel ran across the hay and up a tree. A woodchuck scampered across the field towards the woods and under a fence. On the west and south, the land was mostly level and covered with fields of oats, hay, and garden patches of potatoes, corn, tomatoes, carrots, onions, beets, radishes, and cabbage.

Bernie thought about Marigold. She was twenty-four years old, sturdy and slim. He had known her for quite a while.

He finished the hay raking and halted to unhook the rake from the tractor. He then walked to the end of the driveway to get the mail from the box. He looked at two letters for him; both were bills.

"Mother fuck, I never get any good mail," he said.

Bernie took the mail into the house, and Anna had the noon meal prepared.

"On the farm, every meal is a banquet," stated Ben.

On the table was pie from their apple trees, pork chops from their own pigs, corn from the garden, milk from their cows, homemade bread, and butter from the local creamery. They listened to Paul Harvey give the news and commentary on a tan-colored radio.

Ben belched after the meal and rubbed the food hanging on his mouth.

He never said much at the table because eating was a full-time job. Ben sat crooked on his chair and placed one arm on the far side of his dish and bent over while eating. This farmer did not eat like an Army cadet at a military academy -- they eat while sitting up straight at the table.

Ben looked at a newspaper to see who had died and then walked out while scratching his crotch. He had not used enough toilet paper on his last trip to the bathroom or barn gutter. He wore a blue work shirt and a blue denim bib overall and leather work shoes.

When he was ten yards from the house, Ben emitted a loud cannon fart. The blast scared Neptune, the dog. Ben put water in the tractor radiator and checked the oil. Bernie greased the hay baler. It was a red New Holland baler. Bernie worked hard stacking the bales onto a wagon, and he was sweating.

"We need some help in the barn," said Ben. "I will call Steve and ask if he will help us out. We just can't dump those hay bales in the haymow because someone has to stack them."

Ben made the telephone call from a black rotary phone in the milk house. Dark thunderclouds were forming in the east, so the hay harvest might have to be postponed.

Chapter Three

Chester Borseth, Louie, and their dad, Ole, had gone to town for some machine parts. Lucy had stayed home to can corn. While opening a dresser drawer to replace some clean socks in Chester's room, she espied some gold coins.

Upon examining them, she said, "These coins have the date of 1873. My goodness, I wonder where my boy found this money?" She put them back in the drawer.

That night at the supper table, Chester was reading a new comic book entitled, Straight Arrow; it was about the Comanche Indians. Lucy was putting food on the table.

"Where did you find these gold coins?" she asked while showing them in her hand.

Being a bit surprised, he pondered a moment. "I found them in the woods in a metal box," replied Chester. He did not want to say too much as yet since it was still a secret.

"Well, put them in a safe place because those twenty- dollar gold coins are worth more today," Lucy added.

"Don't tell Louie and Ole," he pleaded.

The next morning after Chester had finished feeding the chickens and ducks, his pal Rusty appeared on a bicycle in the driveway.

"Let's go back to that cave to search again for that treasure soon," said Rusty.

Summer Mirage

"I have been thinking about that. Lucy knows I found some coins, but she knows nothing else," stated Chester.

The two friends mounted their Monarch bikes and sped down the driveway. High stratus clouds were floating in the sky above. Some farmers were putting up their second crops of hay. The teenagers entered the Woodward farm and saw nobody around.

"Old man Woodward will not mind if we explore his cave again," said Chester.

"I do not trust his strange son Clyde because he keeps mostly to himself," commented Rusty.

They parked the bikes by the grove of trees next to the cave. Unknown to them, Clyde was watching them from a barn door with a pair of binoculars. He blew a wad of green snot onto the barn floor, farmer style, by holding a finger to his nose.

"I wonder what Chester Borseth and Rusty Wampauch are up to," pondered Clyde.

Rusty tied a rope to a tree trunk so they could lower themselves into the steep entrance. A cottontail rabbit hurried up the path, scared by the intruders. Searching the far wall with a flashlight, they saw more Indian paintings.

"We missed this the last time," said Chester.

"I will start digging this time," replied Rusty. He worked with the spade digging up the sand on the cave floor. Chester searched further into the cave.

"The cave narrows back in here," he motioned. He could not be sure if the bones he saw were animal or human. "I wonder what the Indians looked like who entered here first?"

"Yeah, were they Sioux, Iowa, or Winnebago?" replied Rusty.

"Hey, I just found two Indian arrowheads," yelled Chester in surprise.

Rusty dropped his shovel to marvel at the discovery.

After a while, Chester took his turn at the digging. Just when he was ready to give up, he heard a clink on the shovel. He dug some more. It was a box that felt heavy as Chester lifted it up to take a look.

He lifted the cover as Rusty held the light in place. The boys were all smiles as they grabbed the gold coins.

"This is our lucky day," laughed Rusty.

"I hope we can hold on to this treasure," said Chester. "There may be three hundred seventy twenty-dollar gold pieces in the box, plus the five we found before, would total seventy-five hundred dollars, just as Jesse and Frank James wrote on that paper," he added.

"Let's wait to count it when we get home," suggested Rusty.

"Well, we made a mistake. This box is too heavy to carry on our bicycles; we will have to return on our horses to get this out," explained Chester.

The two adventurers climbed back up to their bikes and sped away towards their homes. Clyde had kept watching the whole time.

He walked the two hundred yards from his barn to the cave.

"I see they forgot their rope here tied to a tree," he said to his collie dog that was trailing along. Clyde slid down the rope to the entrance and walked inside the cave. He espied the box of gold coins lying on the floor.

"God almighty," he exclaimed in surprise.

"Where are you boys riding to now?" asked Louie as his brother and Rusty were mounted back at the Borseth farm.

"We are just exercising the horses," replied Chester.

"Maybe I will come along on my strawberry roan, Dick," replied Louie, who was eager to join the group.

"Join us next time," said Chester.

Upon reaching the cave again, Rusty and Chester slid on the rope to the entrance. With their flashlights shining, they came to the site where they had left the treasure box.

"It is gone. This is starting to become a mystery," exclaimed Rusty.

They looked for tracks on the sandy floor.

"Look, tracks different from our cowboy boots," said Rusty.

"They could be tennis shoes," concluded Chester.

"They will most likely be Clyde's," said Rusty as they made their way back up the cave entrance.

"Let us head for home now and figure out what to do next. We can return to spy on Clyde and maybe discover where he hid that box. Maybe we need the help of Louie and Sam, our brothers," stated Chester.

The earth had rotated a couple of times, and back on the east side of the Mississippi River, the Bakers were still busy with the hay harvest. They had hired Steve, about thirty, with dark hair; he was handsome. He climbed the hay chute inside the barn to stack the hay bales, and it was hot upstairs.

They got in many loads of hay that day; the cattle would not go hungry over the long winter looming ahead. The table talk at night was the usual kind for farmers. They discussed the crop yields and whether or not they would finish before it rained.

After the talking and eating, Steve left for home. The Bakers gathered around the television set. That night, Ben, Anna, and Bernie looked at, "Your Hit Parade," starring the singers Gisele McKenzie and Dorothy Collins, the brunette and the blonde. Then an Alfred Hitchcock mystery appeared on the tube, followed by an episode of "Dragnet," starring fast-paced Jack Webb and Ben Alexander, along with piano music. The family soon drifted off to bed.

It was Saturday, and Bernie was waiting for Marigold to call on him. The hours dragged by as he waited at the picnic table.

His dog Neptune enjoyed being petted while wagging its tail.

I think I will drive by her farm, Bernie thought. He sped off in his green 1949 Chevrolet and soon espied her sitting under a tree next to Steve. He had his arm around her.

I wonder what she is up to? he thought. Bernie then stopped at the old General Store and had a snack.

The old clerk was playing a card game of solitaire. The two men discussed the weather and the local news. The clerk stood up to blow a book-slamming fart.

Later, Bernie drove home and parked his Chevy under a tree. The dog was waiting and wagging his tail.

"You can't trust anyone these days," Bernie sighed.

On Sunday, Bernie attended church in La Crosse with his parents. Marigold arrived at the same time.

"Howdy, neighbor," greeted Bernie. "I expected you to visit me yesterday."

"I had house cleaning to do," she explained.

"I thought you did your spring cleaning last April," he replied.

"There is always some cleaning to do." They sat together in a booth while the pastor talked.

"The father brings his son into a bar and orders whiskey for himself and a sucker for the child. You should live as good a life during the week as you do on Sunday."

Marigold was listening, but Bernie was falling asleep.

"How about a date Wednesday night?" asked Bernie as the sermon ended. He was testing her.

"Okay. I also got a new job at the agricultural office."

"That is great," replied her friend. All seemed fine.

The next day, Ben said to his son, "Anna and I are going to La Crosse, so I called up Steve to help you stack hay bales in the hay loft. Anna is clearing off the table."

Okay, I will get started now," said Bernie.

Ben and his wife drove out of the yard in their new gold-colored Chevy. While walking to the barn, Bernie thought he saw a mirage of a grove of trees glimmering over the pond in the heat of the day.

"I thought mirages only occurred in deserts," said Bernie.

Steve arrived and climbed the hay chute. "Yes, sir," he greeted Bernie. He wore bib overalls.

"I am done on the east end of the barn, so let's get started on the other end and try to finish today," said Bernie.

After an hour passed by, Bernie said, "I am hotter than hell, and I'm heading for the house to fetch us some beer to cool off with."

"A good idea," replied Steve. He was a little younger than Bernie, and both were good workers.

Bernie climbed down the hay chute and some chaff followed him. He stopped to brush it off his shirt.

At the house, Bernie drank a swig of Sunnybrook whiskey, and then grabbed two beers with Schlitz labels. Upon returning to the hayloft, he handed a can to Steve.

"That really hits the spot," Steve smiled.

"And one hour later it hits the pot," Bernie retorted.

Soon, the two men continued working in the hot loft. Bernie was higher up in the haymow than Steve, and suddenly when Steve's back was turned, a bale of hay hit him, and he fell over.

"I am sorry," said Bernie. He continued working.

"Be more careful," Steve replied, a frown on his face.

Some ten minutes later, as Steve was putting a bale into place, another struck him from behind.

"God damn it, watch it," warned Steve. He was hot both from working and from anger.

In another short while, Bernie released a big bale of hay with its green fresh bulk and it rolled and bounced, hitting Steve as he turned around. He collapsed with the bale on top of him. He was red in the face upon rising.

"By damn, you did that on purpose, and I am going to castrate you today," stated Steve in a fury. He approached Bernie with a knife.

Bernie edged backwards, hardly believing his eyes. He fell into a crevice in the hay bales.

Steve loomed closer with his shiny blade of steel. It could soon have stains of red on it. As he was about to plunge with his ugly pig sticker, Bernie jerked out a pearl-handled derringer from his pocket and bored his opponent in the chest.

"You are not cutting me, you lousy woman stealer," shouted Bernie.

In anger, Steve's eyes almost popped out as he dropped his knife and threw up his hands as if catching a football; he fell back with a groan. Bernie's anger turned to fright.

He hurried down the hay chute and out of the barn. No one else was home. He walked in a circle.

"What shall I do now? Is he dead?" Bernie questioned. He rushed back up the hayloft and saw the ghastly form of Steve stretched out on the hay bales. He was as dead as a dusty mummy in a pyramid.

Bernie then talked in a soliloquy.

"What should I do with him? I could call the sheriff, but he might not believe it was self-defense. Steve was monkeying around with my girl, and I should feed him to the pigs; he does deserve it. Or, should I bury him in the God damn barnyard and dump a load of bullshit on top of him to hide it? I could wrap him in canvass and tie rocks on his arms and legs to sink him into the deep pond. No nosey person would find him then." He stared at the body. "By shits, I know what I will do with the corpse, and I will have to move fast." He started dragging the body out of the barn.

It was night in the upper Midwest, and the rain was coming down in buckets. Ben and Anna were driving home from a shopping trip to La Crosse. There was thunder and lightning as a skunk ran onto the road, and the car wheels passed over the stinker, squirting its guts out like toothpaste from a tube.

As they entered the driveway, Ben broke the silence by saying, "That's funny, there are not any lights on in the house or in the barn."

"Maybe Bernie went to Hokah or La Crosse after doing the chores," replied Anna.

As they entered the house, she flipped the light switch. "There are not any lights, Ben; the juice is out because of the storm."

"The hell you say!"

Anna lit two candles, while Ben went to the barn with a lantern. Later, he returned to the wood frame, two-story house. Ben removed his straw hat.

"Bernie must have gone some place since the cows are still outside. You have to help me with the chores."

The couple headed for the barn where Ben put feed in front of the stall while Anna put the milking machines together in the milk house.

Ben climbed the hay chute. "The job of hay stacking is not done. I will have to ask Bernie what he has been up to. Maybe Steve did not come today."

After they got the cows into the barn, Anna grabbed the egg basket to fetch the eggs. Ben entered the granary and fetched a pail of ground oats and corn and carried it into the pigpen.

Damn, it's dark in here. I will have to get the lantern from the barn, he said to himself.

The rain was still coming down. The sky was pitch black and walking with a lantern made fleeting shadows or phantoms. He returned to the pigpen and entered the sliding door where he lowered the lantern over the partition. Ben Baker was in a state of horror.

"Good God! A body being chewed on by my hogs!" He hurried out the door just as Anna exited the chicken coop.

"Anna, there is a body in the pigpen all covered with shit and blood. I don't know who it is, but I don't think it's our son."

She set down the egg pail.

"Oh, heavens!" she responded.

They rushed to the house and called the fat county sheriff. The lawman and a deputy arrived within a half hour.

"It might take a while before we can determine if there has been foul play," the sheriff, with his middle-aged bulge, said. He dragged the corpse into the milk house to wash off the body.

"It's Steve, a neighbor!" said Ben. "He was here today to help Bernie stack hay bales."

"Where is Bernie?" asked the sheriff.

"I have not seen him since I left for town early this morning," Ben replied.

The deputy unbuttoned the shirt on the dead man.

"That looks like a bullet hole," he concluded quickly. "This is big trouble, and I will take this stiff to town, but we will be back," stated the lawman.

"The hogs did not damage the body," said the sheriff.

"That is because they are used to a diet of corn and oats," said Ben.

The lawman wrapped the body in a plastic bag and carried it to his car and left.

The juice came on again, and the lights were working. Anna came and Ben told her of the events. "Bernie must be innocent, and we have to hope for the best," he told her.

Anna appeared worried. She wore a pink scarf over her brown hair and held an umbrella. The lady was a fair-looking woman over fifty.

"You can help me with the milking if you are able," said Ben.

They started with the work.

After Bernie had dumped Steve's body into the pigpen, he lit out on foot for a cave two miles away.

Chapter Four

Bernie had a dinner pail and had stuffed it full of food before his flight. Nobody had seen him in his trek across the fields. Inside the cool cave, Bernie huddled.

"I should be safe here since nobody will think of looking for me in this cave," he said. He saw writing carved into the sandstone on the cave wall. One was "George, 1880." Next to a wall lay an old rusty bicycle.

Close to the entrance lay the bones of a bird; perhaps a badger had dragged a chicken inside the cave and had eaten it. On an opposite wall were two black marks, but Bernie could not understand what they meant.

There is a lot of history to this cave, he thought.

Bernie took out a peanut butter sandwich from his old dinner pail. He settled back and relaxed.

The next day, the sheriff and deputy were nosing around up in the hayloft.

"I just found a knife," exclaimed the tall deputy.

"Let me see it!" replied the sheriff with the beer belly. Yeah, let's search some more."

A while later, the fat man said, "Look what I found under this hay bale. A derringer."

"It must be the gun that killed Steve; we will have to check it out," added the deputy.

Later, they showed the weapon to Ben who shook his shaggy head. Soon, they had gone down the road with Ben looking at their trail of dust on the gravel road.

Back at the cave, Bernie was thinking.

"Son-of-a-bitch, I am in hot water now," he soliloquized. "When they find me, they will burn me at the stake, as they did during the Colonial witch hunts three hundred years ago. But wait, it was a matter of him or me, self-defense. He pulled a knife on me, and I shot him to defend myself. Hell, I am going to give myself up," Bernie said.

Bernie climbed out of the cave just as his distant ape-like ancestors had done a million years earlier. Soon, he was strolling past the long familiar wood frame buildings on his home farm. He looked up to see a flock of ducks fly by under the high cirrus clouds. Bernie thought the quacking sounded like Donald Duck.

Anna was outside mowing the lawn, and seeing her son, she called out, "Ben, he is back; it's Bernie!"

Ben emerged from the house to approach his son. "We have been wondering where you were. The nosy sheriff was here on account of Steve being deader than a sun-dried cow pie."

"He pulled a knife on me, and I had to speed a lead slug in his direction. It was self-defense," replied his son.

"The law should go easy on you then," said Anna after she shut off the lawn mower.

"I will go with you to the sheriff's office," Ben told his son.

The farmers drove to the county seat in La Crosse and entered a building. After Bernie told his story again, the uniformed human bull locked Bernie behind bars.

A short time had gone by, and the trial was in action. On a sunny day, Bernie was led into the courtroom. The prosecuting lawyer began to talk. He wore a tan-colored suit.

"This man claims that he killed in self-defense, and yet there was not a witness there to see it. Are we going to take Bernie Baker's word for it, a man with his reputation?" the lawyer questioned the jury.

The attorney for the defense interrupted, "I object to that statement."

"Overruled, now continue with the case," ordered the judge.

"The weapon used to kill Steve Brown was found at the scene in the Baker barn. I urge we find Bernie guilty." The big mouth lawyer took his seat.

Then the defense attorney took his turn on the floor.

"This man claimed he shot only to protect his own life, and I believe him. Bernie is a hard-working man, and I would rather take his word than that of some loafer or vagabond," the young lawyer stated.

"Will you stick to the facts?" the judge said.

"All right. Steve's knife was found at the scene; that proves there was danger for Bernie. I believe he is not guilty of murder," the defense lawyer continued. He took his seat.

Then Bernie was called to the stand.

"Do you swear to tell the whole truth?" the old fart asked.

"Yep, I do," answered the man accused.

The prosecuting attorney finally asked, "How do you account for Steve's body being found in the pigpen that night?"

"It beats the shit out of me," replied Bernie.

"Is that all you have to say for yourself?" the able man retorted.

"The last time I saw Steve was when he was in the hay loft," said Bernie.

"Are you suggesting that Steve went to the pigpen after you shot him?" queried the lawyer.

"You cannot prove how Steve ended up in the company of hogs," Bernie said.

"That is all I have," said the lawyer.

"You may leave the stand, Bernie," said the judge.

The defense lawyer approached the front. "Since we are not able to prove there was a murder here, the only choice is to declare Bernie innocent of any crime," he stated.

Summer Mirage

The proceedings ended when the judge asked for the trial to continue two days later. Bernie was returned to jail.

That night, he played checkers with a prospective deputy. He was a young man who had passed the written and physical tests and had a uniform on.

"How are you at checkers?" Bernie asked his opponent.

"Fair to good," replied Jake. He smoked a pipe while contemplating a move.

Bernie won the first game.

"Good going there, you jailbird," responded Jake. "You should have seen me when I took the agility test. I did thirty sit-ups and ran the one-hundred-yard dash in good time," added Jake.

"Great, but what's that to me?" said Bernie as he jumped three of Jake's red pieces with a king. Bernie won the second game too, using the sheriff's expensive wooden set.

The jailer and prisoner drank brandy together.

The jury and others in the case gathered again soon.

The judge said, "You have heard the lawyers and the defendant speak, and now you people in the jury are to leave the room and come back when you all have reached a verdict."

The men and women went to a back room to consider the case. It seemed like a long time for the Baker family. Finally, they returned to the courtroom.

"How do you find the defendant?" asked the old fart.

"Bernie is innocent of all charges!" a man, who was standing and speaking for the jury, stated.

Ben and Anna hugged each other in joy. Bernie stood up and shook hands with his lawyer. Newspaper and radio reporters were on the scene, and a courtroom artist was on hand for the dramatic event. The Bakers walked outside.

As Bernie was nearing his car, he said to himself, Son-of-a-bitch, I missed that date with Marigold Clausen. I guess I will go and see her. He went to a saloon first and drank two glasses of Bub's beer for fifteen cents each.

"I wonder if my dog, Neptune, still remembers me after I have been gone a few days?" he asked the cute blonde bartender.

"He might if you shake hands with him," she curtly replied.

"You look seductive in those blue Bermuda shorts," Bernie commented. Later, Bernie was on the road going towards the farm home of his girlfriend.

As he approached, he saw her carrying a milk pail from the milk house to the barn. She was wearing a cool yellow blouse and shorts. He parked beside the red milk house.

"Are you doing the milking tonight?" asked Bernie when she was near the barn door.

"No, I just help my dad get started; he is inside busy with the milking now," replied Marigold.

"How about going to a movie tonight?" Bernie suggested.

She did not reply as they strolled towards the house. She was pondering the idea. "I don't think so. That trouble you were in bothers me."

"The past is dead; let's forget all about it and the trial of late," said Bernie.

"Maybe soon," she replied.

"Okay, I will be seeing you," he added.

The country damsel entered her house, and Bernie got into his car, taking Road Sixteen for Hokah. He entered a saloon and sat a long time drinking beer.

"God damn, she stood me up tonight. Oh, well, Steve will not monkey with her anymore because I eliminated that bastard."

The bartender was a pretty redhead wearing a pink blouse and green skirt. "Do you want another beer now?" Renata asked him.

"Yeah, bring me a bottle of Hamm's," replied Bernie."How about a date tonight?" he added.

"Not tonight farm boy, I already got one," she said.

"I feel like going places tonight." He left and said goodbye to the other barflies and swung back onto Road Sixteen.

He drove west and entered Rushford, bordering Root River and bluffs of hardwood trees. Bernie entered the Trojan Theater to see the movie Gone With the Wind, starring Vivian Leigh. He visited the snack bar for a hot dog and a Seven-Up, and the waitress was talkative.

"Do you like the movie?" she asked.

"I don't know; I did not taste it yet!" replied Bernie.

"Ha, ha, ha!" she laughed.

He enjoyed the show and laughed when Butterfly McQueen talked about birthing babies.

As he was driving home, a dumb cat walked across the road. It reacted too slowly, and the wheels passed over him. Its eyes and brains squirted out, like one squirts out hair tonic from a tube.

Bernie laughed. "By shits, I got him, ha, ha, ha." He figured there was a cat overpopulation.

He entered the windbreak at his farm home, and Neptune, the short-tailed English shepherd, greeted him.

He petted man's best friend and wrestled and rolled over with his dog. There was an afterglow of the sunset.

"I wish Marigold had gone with me to the movie," he said.

The following day, back at the Borseth and Wampuch farms, not far from Rushford where Bernie had been, Chester and Rusty had enlisted the aid of their brothers to reclaim the treasure. The foursome was standing under a tall oak tree.

"If we get those gold coins back, we will divide it four ways," said Chester.

"That sounds good!" spoke his brother, Louie.

"I do not know what I will do with the money," added Sam, the younger brother of Rusty.

"Here is the deal; we will take turns by spying on Clyde with my binoculars. We can ride our bikes to the Woodward farm and stay undercover," explained Rusty. He always had good ideas, and that one might pay off.

Louie mounted his bicycle and said, "I will spy first."

"If you discover where the box of coins is, come back and tell us. We will need to haul it back on a horse," said Chester.

They watched him ride down the road.

Later, Louie was hiding in a grove of trees watching the farm of Clyde. The strange youth exited the house and went near a woodshed to take a leak.

Ha, ha, ha, he is watering the lawn! said Louie to himself. Then Clyde walked to the granary nearby.

Louie quickly ran to the site under cover of trees. He peeked through an open window to see Clyde lift up two feed sacks and open the cover of the treasure box.

"I am a rich boy now!" said Clyde with a smile on his homely face.

Louie quickly retreated to his bike and sped away home. Chester was in the dairy barn putting ground feed for the cows in front of their stanchions when Louie came.

"Clyde has the treasure, and it's in their granary!" said Louie excitedly.

"Tell me all about it!" replied Chester. He heard the details and then said, "We will go for the gold tonight."

At dusk, as the gold and purple sunset stared at the four youths, Louie mounted his strawberry roan, Dick; Chester was on his sturdy horse, Fury; Rusty was on his bay, Tony, and Sam was on a sorrel, Wildfire. All were speedy quarter horses, and Chester's palomino was the most colorful, but that could be argued.

They trotted over the dirt road towards the Woodward farm. As the sky darkened, they reached a grove of oak and elm trees bordering the farm.

"Their dog sleeps in the barn at night, so we won't have to worry about him barking," said Louie, feeling important in their adventure.

"I will walk with Louie, and we can take Wildfire along to carry back the box of gold coins," said Sam.

The four teenagers agreed on the plan.

"I hope they will not make much noise," said Chester.

He and Rusty watched them walk towards the granary in a pale moonlight.

"Look, there goes old man Woodward and his wife out of the driveway in their car!" said Rusty.

Summer Mirage

"Oh, oh, there goes Clyde walking from the barn to the granary. We have to hurry to the aid of our brothers," added Chester.

They tethered their horses to a tree and raced for the granary. Clyde sneaked up to the granary holding a .22 rifle squirrel gun with a telescope.

"I caught you two trespassers now!" uttered Clyde, and Louie and Sam turned around.

"Put your gun down, you dumb idiot; this is not the wild West," said Sam, who was smarter than he usually pretended to be.

"He would be stupid enough to shoot," said Louie, who was usually rather quiet.

At that moment, Rusty came up behind Clyde and hit him on the head with a baseball bat. The latter saw a galaxy of stars and tipped over like a sack of potatoes.

"I did not hit him very hard, so he will be all right," said Rusty.

"He will not remember much when he wakes up," added Chester.

Louie closed the cover on the box of treasure and with the help of Sam, carried it to his mount, Wildfire. They secured the box with ropes. The foursome hurried to the grove of trees; and when all four were mounted, they made dust for their home farms.

The next day, they gathered at a favorite spot in the woods to count and divide up the twenty-dollar gold coins. They each had feed sacks to carry the money. Their happy faces told the story with their smiles.

"Rusty and I might use our shares for college," said the oldest boy, Chester.

"Louie and I are still thinking how to spend our shares," put in Sam.

When the counting was done, they all got in Chester's dark blue, 1952 Chevrolet and took the road for Winona.

The youths entered the marble stone Merchants National Bank with their treasure.

After seeing the gold coins, the fat, pink-faced cashier put down his cigarette. "This money is now triple the value, $22,500. You farmers are now rich!" the chain smoker said.

"Happy days are here again," smiled Rusty.

"We will still have to work though," added Louie, who was sometimes a pessimist.

The foursome exchanged the old gold coins for current-day money, and each deposited his shares in savings accounts.

Chapter Five

During the next few days, Ben and Bernie got the annual job of haying done. The fine weather had stayed clear, and the rustic farmers harvested corn, oats, and hay. Some of them put clover and alfalfa into their concrete silos when it was still freshly cut and green.

It was Saturday, and Bernie made a call on the black rotary telephone to his neighbor, Marigold.

"Are you free and loose tonight?" he asked.

"I am as loose as a goose," she replied.

"Okay, I will be over to see you." He soon approached the Clausen spread, a neat farm with the fields and buildings on a level grade of land. Most of the sheds were painted white, and a windbreak of fir and pine trees protected the homestead in the winter. Her family raised Holstein cattle and white Leghorn chickens. White, fluffy cumulus clouds sailed above.

As Bernie entered the yard, the family dog, a German shepherd, rushed up, curious about the visitor.

"Howdy, Mars," he said as he petted her. Marigold was on a porch sitting down. "Hello," said Bernie upon nearing her.

"Hi, let's walk to the other side of the house," she said.

"Okay, you are the boss."

They strolled over to a large oak tree, which may have been planted when Rutherford Hayes was President, and they sat down on the green lawn. There were a couple of robins close by prancing about looking for worms or bugs.

"I am calling off our engagement, so here is your ring back," the blonde damsel stated soberly.

"What is the big idea?" he asked curiously.

"I cannot marry anyone who has killed a person. If it had been in a war, that would be different," said Marigold.

"So that's it," replied Bernie.

"I am not going out with you anymore," she added.

"And all those times we were together, in the straw pile, at the movies, and the picnic last summer!" Bernie reminded her.

"I am sorry," she said. The farmer's daughter got up and walked back to the house.

Bernie sat there dumbfounded a while before leaving. He did not feel well, as things had gone contrary to his liking. He drove to the village of La Crescent and sat by a curb where he saw a sign, "Hamm's and Liquors."

He entered the bar and heard the country tune, "Seven Lonely Days," sung by Kitty Wells. A man sitting next to Bernie had just returned from the Korean War.

"Did you see any action over there in Harry Truman's War?" the pretty bartender asked.

"Oh, hell, yes. I shot four gooks and eight chinks with their beady eyes," the macho veteran stated.

"Good for you, and here is a drink on the house," said Lisa. "How did you feel about boring those foreigners with hot lead?"

"It was no different from shooting a pig," said the man.

"Give me another bottle of Hamm's beer," demanded Bernie.

"Don't get your water hot!" replied Lisa.

The Crystal Palace saloon was a classy place. He continued getting drunk, and every time he ordered a drink, he did not get change back. Bernie was a sucker being taken by Lisa who was cheating him.

A fool and his money soon part, she thought while pouring drinks.

After sipping on a shot of Sunnybrook bourbon whiskey, he staggered out to his green, 1950 Chevy that he had gotten recently.

He fell asleep in the back seat. The cool Minnesota night was made for a relaxing slumber. He heard frogs and crickets.

It was getting light in the east with the full moon going down in the west when Bernie got up. He fumbled for his keys, turned the engine on and drove home. Upon arriving, he helped in the barn with milking the cows, slopping the hogs, and doing the utensils in the milkhouse. Bernie watched TV on the black and white screen while his parents attended church.

"I got nothing to praise God for today," he said.

His folks were gone all day visiting relatives while Bernie watched a film on the boob tube or idiot box. It was Roy Rogers and John Wayne in the movie Dark Command, with pretty Claire Trevor as the live bait.

That night, he drove to La Crescent and parked next to a saloon. Bernie found a stool and lit up a Chesterfield cigarette. He had begun smoking that brand after baseball stars had endorsed the product in magazine ads and on television.

"Hey, aren't you going to say hi to me?" a familiar voice said.

The farmer jerked his head around and recognized Sally Benson, a brunette.

"Meet my new friend, John," she said.

"Hi, pal!" he said to the man in a sport shirt. He had a brown mustache and was average looking.

"Where is your lady friend tonight?" asked Sally.

"I do not have a fiancée any longer," responded Bernie.

"Who broke it off, you or Marigold?" the well-shaped lady queried.

"If I tell you everything, you will know more than me," he retorted.

The tune being played on the jukebox was "Why Don't You Believe Me," sung by Joni James. Bernie and John, an educated man, discussed sports.

"Do you think the New York Yankees or the Milwaukee Braves will win the title this year?" asked John.

"It don't make any difference to me who wins because it's no money in my pocket. I don't give a damn if a whole team died in an airplane crash," stated Bernie.

"Don't you like any sports?" asked John.

"I follow the high school football teams like La Crosse, Hokah, and the Trojans of Rushford."

"We have to be going," said Sally while looking at John.

"So long my friends," spoke Bernie.

After they had left, he got drunk again. It seemed as though he wanted to forget things.

Two male bartenders were serving drinks along a long bar.

"Look at that drunk stud over there!" said one as he motioned towards the farmer.

"Let's take him," replied the other.

They gave Bernie more beer and cheated him out of his money. The night dragged on with a nearly full moon shining brightly. Bernie knew where the first $20 went, but not the next $50. It slowly slipped away into the greedy, soft white hands of the city slickers.

Bernie staggered back to his Chevy car and drove out of town. The town cop was as blind as a bat and did not notice Bernie driving funny. He parked his car within sight of the Mississippi River and walked to the ditch to pass some water. Suddenly, his car drifted down a slope and crashed into an elm tree. Bernie had forgotten to put on the emergency brake.

"By shits, everything happens to me!" He got in his wreck and was soon asleep.

The next day, a brown highway patrol car stopped when the uniformed officer saw the odd accident. He came near the scene and espied Bernie on his back. The windows were open, and he had puked on the floor. The law officer awakened Bernie and led him to a patrol car.

"Where do you live?" asked the pompous advanced ape.

"Go down that road a few miles, and I will show you," said Bernie.

They were soon at the Baker farm, and Bernie walked to the house. He felt wearisome.

"I radioed in for a wrecker, and we will tend to your car," said the officer as he left.

Bernie entered the kitchen.

"You have been absent a lot from work," said Ben.

"That's tough shit," replied his son.

"We do not need you anymore, so hit the road," he said, and he shoved Bernie.

The latter had a hangover, but he still had strength. He gave his dad a punch in the belly, and Ben toppled to the floor, clutching his midsection. Anna was outside picking eggs in the chicken coop. Bernie went upstairs, packed his suitcase, and walked out to the road. He hitchhiked a ride in a pickup truck being driven by a farmer.

"Where are you headed for, neighbor?" he asked.

"The sleepy hamlet with all the stores on one side of the street, cute Lewiston."

Meanwhile, Anna had returned to her house with a basket of eggs. Ben looked somewhat downhearted.

"Bernie and I had an argument, and he left with a suitcase."

"Some time away from home is good for the soul," replied the wise lady of the house. She set about packing eggs in a box.

Bernie and the other farmer made a stop at the Wyattville store for soda pop.

"This is great farming land," observed the farmer, Brent.

"The hell you say," replied Bernie.

The tune "Tweedlede-Dum," by Laverne Baker was playing on a jukebox, then "Cherry Pink and Apple Blossom White," by Perez Prado. Two odd-looking bachelors, named Archie and Dave, who were wearing felt hats, were at the bar drinking Royal Crown Cola.

"How far is it to Lewiston?" asked Bernie.

"About seven miles," replied Archie.

Some time later, the Borseths were putting in a barn cleaner and a new milk house with a bulk tank on their farm in Minnesota. They had dairy cattle, chickens, and ducks. The nice fields were mostly level with some rolling areas. Leslie Grey, a brother-in-law of Chester's, had just hired a new man.

Les was selling some hogs at the Lewiston sales barn, and afterwards, he saw a man standing in front of the White Knight Saloon. He seemed to be unemployed, and since Les needed a hired man, he asked the stranger if he needed a job. The man accepted work for $175 a month, plus free room and meals. That was a good deal at the time. Bernie Baker had said he had good farm experience in Wisconsin.

Bernie appeared to be near forty, and his nose was a little crooked, probably from being in barroom brawls. Les soon saw that Bernie was a good worker.

"The harder I work, the better I feel," he had once said.

The other man that Leslie recently had had was not worth the powder to blow him to 'billy hell. Art, the fart, had been slower than molasses in January.

Ole and Chester were shoveling out the cow manure and bullshit when they espied Bernie. He was in a white shirt and a bib overall; he was about medium height and well built with well-developed arms and brown hair.

Chester too was medium in height, had brown hair, and was a little on the slim side.

Ole was still fat with gray hair at the temples.

The men started pounding out the floor of concrete for the new barn cleaner.

Later on, Ole left for town, and Chester was in the barn. Since he was the son of the landowner, Chester said to Bernie and Hank, the other laborer from Wisconsin, "When Dad's not here, I am boss."

"You are just a kid," replied Bernie.

"I am a tough kid!" said the other.

"All kids think they are tough," retorted Bernie.

Chester continued his daily chores knowing that Bernie would not be easy to get along with.

The youth climbed a hay chute to throw down straw and hay for the bull and calves.

When Chester was at the third chute heaving down straw with a pitchfork for bedding, Bernie shouted. "Stop that! Stop making all that dust!"

Chester continued finishing the job. "What is a little dust anyway? Ole says dust is good for a person."

Bernie got madder. "God damn it, stop that!" he demanded.

Chester climbed down the hay chute like a monkey to spread out the straw from the oats crop.

"Are you feeding the calves straw?" asked Bernie.

"Yeah, a little straw in their diet is good for them," Chester noted.

"A little straw in your diet would be good for you too," retorted the hired man as he chuckled.

Later, Ole and Chester took the 1939 "B" John Deere tractor and rubber-wheeled wagon to the rock pile to gather rocks to mix with the water, sand, and cement to make concrete. Ole found a whiskey bottle that had been lying outside for years with the cap off and some liquid in it. He lifted the bottle and drank it.

"You should have looked at that water with a microscope first to see what was in it," said his son.

"I wish you had not said that," he replied. Ole also found a comb lying in some garbage, and he picked it up to comb his hair.

As Chester went to crank the tractor by hand, he heard a loud noise, which resembled a shot. Then he realized that as Ole was bending over to pick up a big rock, he had blown a cannon fart. Ole had recently eaten beans and had drunk beer. If he had been standing behind him, he might have been a casualty.

While driving the old green and yellow tractor, Chester knocked down bull thistles on the way to the barnyard. The bull and Canadian thistles were weeds and did not look good on the pasture.

Back by the barn, the farmers unloaded stones from the wagon, and then Bernie and Chester shoveled sand into the mixer. It was hard work, but muscle building.

The next day, Chester took a day off from work to go on a tour with the school kids and a female teacher from a local country school. It was a one-room school with one teacher and twenty children.

Carrol P. Peterson

The sun rose in a golden glow among the purple clouds, and it shone across the river and wooded bluffs. Chester rose early and drove to the railroad depot at Winona. The group boarded a Burlington train bound for St. Paul. Everyone enjoyed the ride. It was late March, and buds were forming on trees.

It was a splendid day in the big city. Maybe Chester was feeling good because of that treasure he had found with his friends, Rusty and Sam. Louie had stayed home on this day.

The first thing the group did was have breakfast. Chester had three big pancakes, Kellogg's Special K, and hot chocolate.

They all felt great as they strolled down University Avenue to the big State Capitol. The tour group watched a live session of the Legislature in progress. Later, they toured the Ford Motor assembly plant. After they visited the Cooperative Midland Building, they rode the train home that night.

The following day, Lucy was packing eggs in the washroom while the men were in the kitchen.

"So you sat by the nice teacher on the train," said Bernie.

"That old whore!" replied Chester.

"That is a heck of a thing to say about a nice old lady," commented Hank. He had no distinctive features on his face or frame.

Bernie appeared a little funny with his crooked nose and bloodshot eyes that stuck out some. He reminded Chester of a black man at the State Fair; he popped his eyes out of his head and jerked them back as one does with the tongue. Only Bernie was a white man and nervous.

After breakfast, Bernie was driving an orange-colored Allis Chalmar's tractor with a scraper mount. He was moving sand, and nobody had ever seen a man drive as he did. He was reckless and backed up and stopped suddenly or would shift gears while still moving, stripping them. The noise that made was loud and had a rhythm to it -- the grinding of the gears and the laboring engine of the tractor. It was like music.

Hank and Chester shoveled sand into the mixer, poured water in with milk pails, and added cement. The mixer circled around while the arms and muscles ached. Over on the gravel road a red Farmall tractor was on the move. It was pulling a plow, and the farmer waved his

Summer Mirage

artificial hand while Chester waved back. He was a neighbor who had had a hand mangled off in a corn picker. It was after three when Lucy brought out lunch.

There were sandwiches of whole wheat, carrot cake, and Bub's beer, brewed in Winona, Minnesota. Chester worked outside until five, then spread feed around for the cows, put the milking units together, and opened the barn door to let the hungry cows in. They were so crazy to eat the feed that Chester ran for safety, or else he would have been trampled by the hoofs of forty head of cows.

Bernie helped lock them up in stanchions. As he touched one heifer on the hindquarter, she kicked him on his knee. He bellowed like a sick maverick that had just eaten locoweed.

"You God damn asshole!" he uttered hoarsely as he twisted the cow's tail and kicked her in the belly. A cow was in the wrong place, so Bernie grabbed a steel pipe and hit her on the head. It worked, and the stupid animal backed up and returned to her rightful stall.

"You kick me again, and I will kill you!" stated Bernie.

They finished milking and then watched television for a while. The family liked to watch "Lawrence Welk" and "Gunsmoke."

The latter show told it like it had been in the American west of the 19th century. The unique American character was formed on the frontier, and that was moving west.

And Mr. Welk, a German American from North Dakota with only a fourth grade education, was richer than most people with university-style degrees. Was he lucky or just smart?

Chester counted the men who got shot on "Gunsmoke," and by the time of the last commercial, nine outlaws had bitten the Kansas dust and had been awarded their one-way vacation trips to Boothill.

Bernie looked at TV intently, and his eyes seemed redder with some wrinkles. He almost looked like a wild man. One had to wonder what his past life had been like. What secrets lay in that shaggy head?

Lucy was the last person up, straining milk and washing eggs for the finicky city women and city slickers.

As Chester lay in an old metal frame bed, he heard the frogs and crickets in the pond and the mooing of a cow. It only seemed a short time, and the sky was purple in the eastern horizon with the dawn.

Carrol P. Peterson

Then a loud noise came from Bernie's room. It sounded as if an encyclopedia was being slammed shut. It was merely a stinking blast from Bernie's anus.

He and Hank had been sleeping in the same bed during the construction of the milk house and barn cleaner on the Ole and Lucy Borseth farm.

Chapter Six

One day they were doing carpentry on the new milk house. Bernie was standing on a sawhorse pounding nails into the roof; it seemed he was thinking of Marilyn Monroe because a thing was projecting from inside his pants. It looked as though he had a carrot inside his levis. It was found out later that Bernie had a rupture.

Chester helped with the construction by sawing wood, nail pounding, shoveling sand, and running the wheelbarrow.

Louie helped also, and he was standing close to Bernie and could see inside his loose bib overall and his bare hinder. It almost looked cute, but he knew it was noisy.

Bernie picked up a large plank of lumber and uttered, "Ahhh." From the seat of his pants came the sound, "Poohh...poop." It sounded as though a dictionary was being slammed shut.

Two salesmen driving a big Buick car, arrived on the scene. One was almost bald and smoked a cigar, and the other looked nervous and spit on the ground every minute while puffing on a Camel cigarette. They wore small town clothes.

"The boss is out with a load of cow shit spreading it on a field," said Bernie.

"We can wait for him," replied Baldy.

"What are you selling?" asked Hank.

"Bulk milk tanks, the best on the market," said the other.

Ole returned and talked to the salesmen.

Carrol P. Peterson

"A bulk tank pays for itself," said the nervous one.

"How can that be?" asked Ole.

"Because the creamery pays you more money for bulk milk than for milk hauled in ten-gallon cans," added Baldy.

"No, shit!" said Ole. "I will buy one."

Then big smiles appeared on the faces of the goofy, greedy salesmen.

Later, Ole left for a town board government meeting. Then another salesman drove into the yard.

"I will get rid of him," said Bernie.

The young dude approached and said, "Would you be interested in our new chicken feed?"

"Shit, hit the road, you city dude," replied Bernie. He slammed the door and went to pounding more nails.

The surprised salesman got the message and sped out of the driveway like a streak of hot shit.

"What time is it?" asked Hank.

"It's pudner four," put in Bernie as he jerked out his pocket watch on a chain.

"I will get us some beer!" said Chester. He jogged to the house and soon returned with three bottles of Kingsbury Beer.

A summer shower came, followed by a rainbow. Later, at dusk, a gold and purple sunset with a silver lining on huge clouds appeared over the woods. It was still May, but it seemed like early summer. On the radio in the barn was heard the song "How Much is that Doggie in the Window," by the singing sensation, Patty Page. Meanwhile, a buck deer jumped over the fence by the woods; and Adolf, the English shepherd, was barking.

Bernie was not seen for a while after the construction job.

It was the lazy, hazy days of summer when Leslie Grey and Bernie arrived at the Ole Borseth farm to help with haying. Ole had cut the clover and alfalfa, and no more cats got their feet cut off in the mower. They would be hunting for field mice; and when the tractor and mower came by, a cat would freeze and not be seen by the driver who had to keep an eye on the path ahead.

The grass was taller than a cat. Ole sped out to chop a load of hay with the Case tractor, and Chester took an empty wagon to join him in a field. The latter was also trapping pocket gophers with his death clutch traps. He halted to inspect a few traps; and as the hired man Bernie put it, one black mound was plugged up tighter than a whore. In the next one, a gopher caught in a trap was snarling.

Chester put a silver tube firecracker under it; and when the fuse went down, the gopher bounced with the blast. The front feet were worth a quarter bounty, and last month he had trapped seventy gophers.

Ole soon had a full load of chopped hay in the green wagon, and he exchanged wagons with his son. Chester sped back to the barn with the full load and parked by the blower.

Bernie was turning the crank on the engine while puffing like a gopher. It was like starting a Model T Ford car. It was started, and they unloaded the hay with forks. The men wore goggles to keep the dusty chaff out of their eyes as the wind was blowing.

Whenever big bunches of hay fell onto the rubber belt, the hay had to be spread out fast or the blower would plug up. It killed the engine.

"Mother fuck! It's plugged up tighter than a toilet!" said Bernie excitedly.

"We will have to unhook the clamp from the pipe," added Les.

The trio dug out the hay from the pipes and inside the orange-colored blower. Chester cranked the engine, and it started.

They soon had the wagon unloaded, and each person knew what to do without anyone giving orders. There were no stupid time clocks on a wall. Between loads, Bernie and his boss, Les, went inside the barn to listen on the radio to the Milwaukee Braves play the Brooklyn Dodgers in baseball on the radio.

Chester returned with another load of chopped hay and asked, "What's the score, Bernie?"

"The Dodgers won nine to seven, and I'd like to kill all of them bums."

"It's only a game," replied the youth.

"Bullshit, I want to see the Braves in the World Series!"

"So do I, and they should win tomorrow because Warren Spahn will pitch for the Braves," stated Chester.

Later, as Bernie was forking off the hay, he put a finger on the side of his nose and blew. A long wad of green snot flew into the hay. Maybe it was good seasoning for the hay, as salt and pepper are to pork and eggs. Les and Bernie were smoking stinking cigarettes, and that would make their arrival at Boothill happen days sooner. Then Bernie dug in his crotch, and it looked as though he was digging for gold. He seemed nervous.

The weather stayed dry, and the haying was finished. It rained, and that gave Bernie a chance to go to town. He got a different car and went to Lang's Bar in Winona. By the time be was half drunk, he noticed that the man sitting next to him was staring.

"What are you looking at me for?" asked Bernie.

"Do you know the difference between a hired man and a pail of horse shit?"

"Hell, no," responded Bernie.

"The pail!" said the other, and he laughed like a hyena.

Bernie rose and socked the joker in his face, knocking him to the floor. "That will teach you!"

The bartender called the cops, and a blue uniformed human bull came. Bernie had spent a lot of money and soon was looking out from behind bars.

The next day, Les came and chatted with the police. Bernie left with Les for the Grey farm, where he would rest up from the hangover. By mid-day, he found a whiskey bottle in his closet and continued drinking. Instead of going to the bathroom, he filled the flower vases with urine; then he found an old coffee pot and filled that each time he got the call of nature. Then he poured it out the window and scared away a cat that was close by. Maybe the cat figured it was a cloudburst.

Summer Mirage

That night, Bernie kept Les and his wife Alice awake by bellowing like a steer. He was having a nightmare, and he saw a dead man sprawled out on hay bales. He had a premonition that a relative of Steve's was looking for him.

Bernie was scared and got up to run for the bathroom, but did not make it in time. He vomited all the way from his door down the aisle. He then took a shower and returned to bed.

He was on a big drunk, and the next day he was drinking wine. Then he staggered outside to sleep in his car.

Chester's older sister, Alice, did not like to have a man lying in her house all day. America had not been built by people lying down all day. The nation had been built on the philosophy of the Puritan and Protestant work ethic, and most farmers were hard workers.

It was a hot day in southeast Minnesota at 95 degrees Fahrenheit. Ole and Chester drove to Les' farm to work on something. The teenager looked at Bernie's car, which was parked in the shade. The windows were open, and there was Bernie on the seat with his head hanging down. He had made a mess in his pants, just as a baby would if it had not been plugged up. He had puked on the car seat and floor. His hot car was full of flies.

Maggots were crawling on the seat of Bernie's pants. Then Chester laughed at the sight because he thought alcoholics were funny. Is Bernie dead or alive? he wondered.

Chester strolled over towards Ole and Les to prepare the grain combine for work. "What kind of tractor is best?" he asked Les.

"They are all made to work," replied his brother-in-law.

It was mid-July, and the oat fields were ready for harvest. Some new parts were needed for the combine and swather, so the trio got into Les' 1953 Oldsmobile and hit the road for the town of Rushford. They passed by the hamlet of Hart.

"There are some damn good farms laid out here," commented Leslie.

The land was level and rich with dark soil, and the cow pastures stayed green all summer. The farm buildings were all well kept up, and the yards were clean as the farmers had the ethnic backgrounds of

Scotch, Irish, German, and Norwegian. Les was letting Chester drive his car, and he passed a truck.

"You should not have passed there," said Les.

"He don't like back seat drivers," said Ole.

"A teenager don't know everything there is to know about driving," added Les.

They entered Rushford where one heard the accent of its Norwegian denizens.

The car crossed Rush Creek and parked on Main Street by a state bank. Les and Ole went to buy machine parts, while Chester visited the Niggle Cafe. There was a good-looking waitress at the counter; she was wearing orange Bermuda shorts.

"I will have a hot fudge sundae," said Chester.

There were two men sitting in a booth talking. "Did you hear about the riot in the city dump last night?" one asked.

"Not yet," replied the other man.

"The dumb farmers were there Christmas shopping!"

They both laughed like hyenas from the jungle.

As the pretty girl was taking Chester's coins, he asked her, "How about a date tonight?"

"I am going steady with someone else," she replied.

He then walked across the street to Hanson's Drug Store to buy a western book, The Lost Wagon Train, by Zane Grey. He read in the car until Ole and Les returned from shopping.

"Do you want to come along to the saloon for a cold soda pop?" asked Ole.

"Yeah, I am dry," replied Chester.

The trio entered the bar and sat on stools around a circular bar. The men ordered a Hamm's beer each, and Chester got a Pepsi-Cola.

On the walls were posters of farm auctions coming up. Land, cattle, poultry, hogs, and grain were sold at those auctions, and good bargains could be made. Gogi Grant was singing "The Wayward Wind" on a jukebox.

Later, they were back at the Les and Alice Grey farm, and Bernie was sobering up. There were whiskey and wine bottles in the barn, in the pigpen, and garage, most being empty. Bernie was sweating, and it seemed as though the alcohol was coming out of his skin. He put the cows in the barn and was moving fast. Maybe he was eager to get back to work.

Bernie had been on a four-day drunk; however, Les had not fired him.

Ole and his son left for their own farm. As they neared a stone bluff quarry, they came upon gravel trucks hauling crushed rock. They were halted for a while by a man standing on the road because they were blasting. He let Ole and Chester pass after the dynamite went off with a bang.

When they arrived home, a man was waiting for them.

"Hi, Howard!" said Ole. "You been waiting for us?"

"Not too long. There is big trouble between two farmers over a fence boundary," replied the other member of the town board.

The men talked in the shade of the garage.

"They are two farmers near Rush Creek, Slim Red and Mr. Belmont. The latter is fencing a strip of land, and Slim Red claims it belongs to him. They both have hot tempers, and I think there is going to be trouble. We have to go and mediate with them," explained Howard.

"Well, we can try and talk some sense into them," replied Ole. "Let's go then!"

Chester went along, and they drove through a windbreak of cedar and fir trees into the Belmont farmyard. Seven dogs came running towards the car. Shirley, his wife, emerged from the white, frame house.

"Come here you stupid dogs and leave the men alone, or I will whip all of you!" she yelled.

The dogs retreated, and Ole, Howard, and Chester confronted the woman.

"Is Belmont home?" queried Howard.

"He went to Chatfield and is not back yet. He must have fallen into a beer barrel," replied Shirley.

"We can come back later," said Ole.

They then went down the road to see Slim Red. They had to avoid hitting the geese, which were fat and slow to move, in the driveway. Slim was cutting weeds with a scythe and did not see the visitors arrive because he was talking to himself. The trio walked to where he was cutting Canadian thistles and poison ivy.

"Good afternoon," greeted Howard, a tall, graying man.

"Howdy, neighbors," answered the farmer with red hair.

"What's this about you and Belmont?"

"That scoundrel is fencing off some of my land, and the dumb rascal thinks he owns it. I went over and tried talking to him, but it was like talking to a fence post," said Slim.

"Won't he even listen to reason?" asked Ole.

"I think his head is all mixed up," replied Slim.

"We were just over there, but all we saw was a pack of mad dogs and his wife," said Ole. "How could Belmont marry a woman like that?"

"He could have done worse," added Chester.

"I don't think so. They are two of a kind, and I am not trying to pull your middle leg either," stated Slim Red with a laugh.

Ole took off his straw bat to wipe some sweat off. "Have you seen a lawyer?" he asked.

"That is a good idea, and I will do that tomorrow," said Slim Red as he dug in his crotch and spit tobacco on the ground.

"We have to get back home to start chores," said Ole.

"When I get this done, I got bull thistles to cut down in the other pasture," said Slim.

As the trio left Slim's farm, they saw his geese wading in the pond. Sometimes there was trouble in pastoral settings.

The next day, after Slim Red had gone to visit a lawyer, he took his scythe and went out to cut thistles and milk weeds in his cow pasture. There were fluffy white clouds in a blue sky, and the moon was not yet visible along the horizon. He walked by a cow path and cut weeds. Sparrows and swallows were flying near the grass and trees. A ground squirrel streaked past a meadowlark and crawled into his hole in a field.

Slim was talking to himself. It's pudner eleven in the morning. Barbara said she would have dinner ready by noon.

He rose at 5:00 a.m. every day and only ate three times a day, not once between meals. He knew that the American Indians ate twice a day, at sunrise and at sunset. The Indians would go to bed with the sun and get up with the sun, always living in harmony with nature. Slim Red was like that, differing from most city folks who did not know when to eat and sleep.

All of a sudden, he sighted Belmont putting up a barbed wire fence on his land. Slim was behind a clump of trees.

"I will show him!" whispered Slim.

He rushed to his barn and got a three-tine pitchfork, and then he returned to confront Belmont. Slim was a tall man of about forty, wearing a straw hat over his red hair, a blue bib overall, and a light blue work shirt.

Belmont was heavy set and average in height. His hobby was blowing long, drawn-out farts. He dressed similarly to Slim.

"What are you doing on my land?" queried Slim.

"This is my land, you skinny shit!" roared Belmont.

"I'll fix ya!" He charged Belmont with the pitchfork, and then Belmont turned around, only to get the sharp steel point in his rear end. He bellowed and ran back to his barn in a rage.

Shirley had gone shopping in town.

"He will never do that again," said Belmont.

He went to his house and put a bandage on his butt. Then he grabbed a gun from a closet. Belmont returned to the site where Slim Red was tearing down the fence.

"I will blow your head off, you silly fart-sucking goofball!" roared Belmont.

Slim dropped his tool and ran for his barn. The armed man pulled the trigger on his twenty-gauge shotgun. Slim was hit in his hinder and legs. He fell to the ground, but rose and continued running. His distance from the blast saved his life.

"By damn, I fixed him!" said the hunter.

Slim called the doctor and the sheriff from a telephone in his milk house. His levis trousers were bloodsoaked.

Chapter Seven

The doctor arrived first and gave Slim Red first aid. The sheriff had been playing cards, and he had drunk too much beer. He had driven into a ditch and had banged up his car. The lawman finally arrived -- three hours after the shooting incident -- along with two deputies in a smashed up Chrysler car.

"I hope you arrest Belmont because he hurt my man," said Barbara, who like her husband was skinny and had red hair. "Now I have to do all the milking myself tonight and slop the hogs. It seems everything happens to us!"

"That's tough shit," replied the fat sheriff.

"We will do our best to apprehend the criminal," added the overweight lawman.

The trio took their leave of Barbara and Slim Red and hurried to the Belmont farm. They walked up to the house to find the door unlocked. A deputy walked in, and the county sheriff followed.

Belmont emerged from a closet and started shooting fast. The first man in a brown uniform and the sheriff both fell dead from the blasts of a double barrel shotgun. Before Belmont could reload his gun, the other lawman entered and fired twice, and the villain fell backwards over a suitcase, arms up-flung into a corner, and things from a shelf fell on top of him.

The fat, ugly deputy inspected the fallen men. All three were deader than doornails.

He talked in a soliloquy. "What should I do now? I can't call the sheriff because there he lies so low and of little significance. It is no use to call an ambulance. Shit, I might as well call an undertaker." He made a telephone call and waited.

On a wall hung a 1953 calendar with big red letters on yellow paper that read: "Rushford State Bank."

Meanwhile, the deputy raided the refrigerator of the Belmont's and consumed two cans of Grain Belt beer and some sardines. He belched so loud that it surprised the big Doberman dog lying by the screen door.

The brown uniformed man or human ape produced a long, drawn-out juicy fart, like a blast from a trumpet. The dark-colored dog shied away to lie under a tree. The wife of Belmont, Shirley, arrived to see three stiffs on the floor.

"So my husband finally met his judgment. I always told him God would punish him some day for all his evil ways, and he got what he deserved," she stated.

"I did not think you would feel that way about it," said the goofy deputy.

"Do you expect me to shed a tear for that fat bastard?"

"For heavens sake, he was your husband."

"Bullshit," replied Shirley, and she meant it.

An undertaker soon came dressed in black clothes; he appeared queer.

"There are two dead fuckers lying by a table and one by that shelf," said the deputy while pointing his finger. "That will keep you busy for a while."

"This is a lucky day for me," said the undertaker. He rubbed his hands and went to work while looking with his queer, greedy eyes.

"Now I have to clean up this mess. Look at all that blood on the floor; damn it anyway, Belmont always leaves a big mess for me to clean up," said Shirley.

The deputy left.

The sun was going down on the Belmont farm as the cows were mooing for feed and waiting to be milked. It was growing dark in the southwest as a storm was brewing, and a strong wind came with rain. There was lightning and thunder, and the rain fell in torrents. A black hearse drove out of the driveway. Shirley, wearing a tan raincoat, opened the barn door to allow the black and white Holstein cows to enter for the daily milking routine. She had to do all the chores alone that evening.

The sun was up with its golden glory as Chester rolled out of bed. He was the first person up on that great summer day except for the farm animals. He was in a good mood because he was going to visit his best friend a few miles down the road. But first he had some work to do.

The white ducks were resting on the grass by the pond, and two wild ones were on the pond swimming. They seemed underfed compared to the tame ducks.

He walked to the barn and the feed room. There were white Leghorn chickens feeding on the ground oats and corn, and they fled as Chester entered. He filled a cart full of feed with a shovel and distributed feed for forty cows. Then he opened a door, but no cattle were in sight.

Could there have been cattle rustlers here in the night? he wondered.

Then he remembered that Ole had put the cows out on fresh pasture yesterday, and they must be grazing on the north forty acres. He saw Adolf lying by the silo door with a yellow cat on top of him. They were good friends.

"Here, Adolf!" yelled Chester.

Adolf jumped up, and the cat went flying.

He called out, "Come, boss!" and the lazy cows started coming home to the red, wood-frame barn that had been built in 1916.

"Sig em!" hollered Chester, and Adolf raced after the lazy and docile ones.

The herd was on the run with the dust floating around.

Ole was standing by the barn door. "Did you have breakfast yet, Chester?"

"Not yet, Dad." He threw a few stones at some heifers, which were reluctant to enter the barn.

Summer Mirage

They soon got all the cattle in their stanchions, and Ole had everything ready for milking. It took about three minutes to milk a cow. At times, a fresh cow would step on a teat, and it became full of blood and garget and posed problems for a milker.

Ole and Chester each ran two Surge milking units. The music of Elvis Presley and "Love Me Tender" were on the barn radio along a wall. In forty minutes they had the herd done and put out to pasture. The youth washed the utensils and went for breakfast. Lucy came with a basket of eggs and put a few on the stove as the men washed up.

Ole was the fastest eater. He sneezed loudly because of all the pepper he put on his eggs, and then he belched as he left the table. As Ole walked out the screen door, he dug in his crotch when he had an itch.

Louie had been going to school and had not been around much during the construction work of the past spring season when Bernie and Hank had been helping at the Borseth farm.

He was down by the pond feeding the ducks. The family had gotten into the habit of not eating at the same time, except on holidays. By the time Ole and Chester had eaten, the younger teenager, Louie, had the wagon loaded with fencing equipment. They wore leather gloves for that work.

Louie shifted into third gear, and they all rode down the lane with Adolf trotting behind in the heat and dust, his tongue hanging out. In the wagon lay a post hole digger, nails, pincher, sledge hammer, barbed wire, fence posts, and a stretcher.

Chester dug the corner post hole while Louie strung out the wire, and Ole pounded the steel posts into the ground. Wooden posts were needed only at the corner of the fence line. The new fence would keep the cattle and horses inside the pasture. The trio soon finished the job, and they returned to the machine shed to unload the fencing tools.

The tractor was as old as Chester. Louie and Ole went to the granary to sack up oats. Chester took the tractor to the manure spreader and cleaned out the calf pens. Afterwards, he climbed the hay chute and threw down straw for the calf bedding.

Next, he cranked the old Case tractor and hauled out the manure onto a field of crops because it made good fertilizer. He saw a lot of pocket gopher mounds, and they reminded him that he and Louie had some trapping to do.

Across the fence, Chester espied his neighbor, Bill, on a Farmall tractor; he was raking straw. They both waved to each other.

Lucy had pork chops, potatoes, and corn on the cob on the table when Chester returned to the house. Ole had raised hogs once, but they had been hard to keep fenced in, so he had sold them.

One time a pig ran through the kitchen, coming through an open door and bursting out a screen door on the opposite side. Lucy did not like to have cats in the house since they ate off the top of the table.

Chester went upstairs to his room and grabbed a suitcase he had packed the night before. They got into the car and started out for the Wampuch farm.

As they neared the yard, a big, barking German Shepherd emerged from a grove of balsam fir trees. Little Cindy was out playing in the yard. Rusty and his folks, Tim and Hilda, came outside to greet all. Rusty, with a straw hat over his red hair, was all smiles. The parents chatted, and Rusty invited Chester inside the white Victorian-style frame house.

"How long can you stay?" he asked.

"Maybe a week or so," said Chester.

"Go up and see Sam who is resting and surprise him," Rusty suggested.

Chester quietly went upstairs and found Sam with a book on his belly. He startled him by grabbing his shoe.

"What the heck? Oh, it's you, Chester; I did not know you had come yet," said Sammy.

They went downstairs.

"I have some good plans! We can take four horses and go camping down by a swimming hole for a couple of days," said Rusty. "Our farm is three hundred acres, and down in the valley is a good swimming place. You, Sam, Cousin Bruce, and myself makes four," explained Rusty.

"Have you seen the horse that Bruce owns?" asked Sam.

"No, not yet," replied Chester.

Summer Mirage

"He has a magnificent white mare that is three years old, and he might come to visit us soon!"

"How old is Bruce?" queried Chester.

"About fifteen and he goes to Rushford High School," Rusty said.

"We can play a game of cards," said Rusty.

The trio sat down at a card table for a few games of wrap poker for pennies. Chester had won a dime when Bruce called up on the telephone. Rusty answered and said they would visit him soon. Hilda then told them to do the chores. The mother was a strong farm lady with brown hair.

The boys went out to carry water to the hogs and chickens. The hens were three kinds of chickens: white Leghorns, Rhode Island Reds, and Plymouth-barred rock. They carried ground feed for the animals.

Later, Sam brought out a BB gun, and they hunted for sparrows and pigeons. Chester had a slingshot along.

The boys knocked a sparrow from a fence and a swallow from a telephone wire line. They entered the red, wood-frame barn and climbed the haymow to seek pigeons. Rusty got one, and they fed the birds to the cat that desired bird meat. Outside, two quarter horses were drinking from the concrete tank, a bay and a strawberry roan. Sam's sorrel, Wildfire, was nearby.

"I own Tony, the bay; do you want to take a ride before supper?" asked Rusty. "You can take the roan."

"Yeah, that will give us a good appetite," replied Chester.

The trio put saddles and bridles on the horses and mounted to ride down the dirt road. They galloped down a shady lane past a white, wood-frame country schoolhouse and a few farms before they turned back. The sun was setting on the horizon, and the purple clouds had a silver lining.

The sky in the far west had a deep gold color, while at the zenith there was a deep blue. In front of them was a field of tall corn seven feet high, and the tassels had spouted. A harvested oats field was seen. Only the short stubs were left.

Sam, Rusty, and Chester raced back to the ranch, galloping past a herd of Black Angus cattle. They rode swiftly down the lane, and the golden rays of the setting sun shone through the grove of fir trees. They thundered into the yard in a cloud of dust.

The horses were hot, and the boy's legs were sore from the riding. While walking to the farmhouse, they smelled the homemade apple pie and baked bread. There was nothing like home cooking. They sat at the table and dug in like hungry teenagers.

Fred, an uncle of Rusty's and Sam's, and a partner on the big farm, was at the table also. He liked to play with and tease little Cindy. The Wampuchs were a happy family.

"How about setting up a tent tonight and sleeping outside? Did you bring a tent along?" asked Rusty.

"I forgot it," replied Chester.

Rusty had good ideas. "I can get three canvasses from the grain binder, and we can bind them together to fashion a tent."

"It is warm out tonight, so let's just lay out a couple of blankets on the cool ground," said Chester.

It was dark when the boys settled down on their blankets for the night. They talked about the good old days when they had attended the country school.

There had been twenty-five students in seven grades with one female teacher. There had been no hot lunch program and no school bus. They each lived a couple of miles from the brick building and traveled by bicycle to classes. Now they were high school students enjoying a summer vacation.

"Our neighbor has had a few cattle missing," said Rusty.

"You mean the Jensens?" asked Chester.

"Yeah, they may have strayed off and got into someone else's herd, or there may be cattle rustlers using trucks," Rusty speculated.

"If that is so, it would not be something new," added Chester.

They were soon lying on their blankets and looking up at the stars. Chester saw something moving in the shadows.

There were deep woods all around them, and he listened and waited. A hairy animal emerged from the bushes; it had shining eyes like red-hot coals. Chester picked up a club lying nearby. Then he realized it was only the big dog, Pluto, a friend. They listened to the sounds of fox and owls down in the valley. Rusty and Chester lay back to relax.

At dawn came the clucking and crowing of the chickens and roosters. They were on time every morning, except they had gotten mixed up once when there had been an eclipse of the sun, and they had gone to roost at mid-day, thinking it was night. It was not known if the roosters were crowing because it was a new day or because they were hungry. The sun was not up yet, and it seemed that a beautiful day was in store.

The boys got the chores done in a jiffy and then smelled the toast from the kitchen.

Hilda was at the stove wearing a green cotton dress. She was a somewhat handsome woman. "Did you brave boys sleep good outside last night?" she asked.

"It was fun, but the dog scared us once when we did not recognize him," replied Rusty.

She poured milk with Wheaties cereal and orange juice. Then came poached eggs and toast.

"Will you help me bring the milk cans to the creamery, Chester, before we visit Bruce?" asked the red-headed teenager.

"Absolutely, I'll help you."

They enjoyed the goodies at breakfast. The men were outside doing farm chores.

"Where is Sam?" asked Chester.

"He is not up yet," said Hilda, as she sat down to eat.

"That lazy bum," choked Rusty with a mouthful of food.

"You watch your language," warned his mother.

Sammy came into the kitchen with sleepy eyes and sat down. The music of Joan Weber singing "Let Me Go, Lover" emanated from a radio.

Chapter Eight

Rusty and Chester drove the Dodge truck to the milk house and loaded up some ten-gallon milk cans. They made the trip to the Wyattville creamery, and then stopped at the general store. They enjoyed bottles of Seven-Up as a farm girl chatted with them. She was a fair-haired damsel.

"Well, look who is here!" said Tamra.

"How are you these days?" queried Chester.

"Just fine and dandy, and what are you boys up to this summer?" She wore blue jeans and a pink blouse.

"I am at Rusty's farm visiting, and we are going on a trip camping."

Both boys wore Levis trousers.

"I wish I could go with you. Just think, we will be juniors in high school this autumn," stated Tamra Hunt.

"Yeah, time flies. What have you been doing lately?" queried Rusty.

"I made a lemon pie this morning. I can see you boys on the hayride this weekend, that is if the wild animals don't get you down in the woods," she responded.

Two old bachelors were sitting at the bar drinking beer.

"You know the one in a brown hat?" asked Chester.

"That is Leighton; he gets real funny when he is drunk, and he swears a lot," said Rusty.

Summer Mirage

"Do you remember when he gave us beer when we stopped on our bicycles at their farm in the forest?" asked Chester.

"Yeah, it was Grain Belt beer, good and cold. Their yard looked like a junk pile."

"One does the cooking, while the other handles the farm work. Ole ate in their house once and had to compete with flies for the food," commented Chester.

Leighton and his wiser brother, Harvey, waved to the teenagers. There were some new posters on the walls of the general store advertising Saturday night dances and farm auctions. A wedding dance with music by the Six Fat Dutchmen was coming up featuring waltzes, polkas, and fox trots. The boys exited out the screen door.

Rusty drove the Dodge truck, and upon reaching the farm yard, Sammy had three horses ready to ride. After carrying the empty milk cans into the cool milk house, they mounted the fast horses and rode out of the driveway before their folks could give them more work to do. There was always something to do on a farm, if only one looked hard enough. The boys were set on having a good time.

It was about two miles to the Bruce Thompson farm, and they raced their horses. Ole had brought over Chester's horse, Fury, the golden palomino, in a truck. Rusty had his bay, Tony, and Sam was on his Wildfire, a sorrel mount. Chester was first, Sam second, and Rusty finished third in the race.

Bruce was in the yard when they entered the gravel road, and he seemed glad to have visitors. Rusty introduced Chester, and they went to the stable. His speedy white mare, Silver, was munching on green hay.

"What kind of horse is that?" queried Sam.

"She is a quarter horse, which is a cross between a mustang and a thoroughbred," bragged Bruce.

"How did you get so smart?" asked Sam.

"I know everything! I am going to race her at the Winona County Fair in St. Charles next year! She is young and can go like a bat out of hell. Do you want to ride her, Chester?"

"I'd be glad to if I don't fall off!"

Bruce slipped a bridle on her head, and he climbed aboard bareback.

Chester discovered that Silver was spirited, and he almost fell off. He rode a short while and then pulled up near the boys and slid off to the ground.

"How do you like her?" asked the owner.

"I wish she was my property. Silver would be easier to control if you put a martingale on her, along with a bridle and saddle," admitted Chester.

"I heard you don't have a tent, Bruce, so we can use our grain binder canvasses for a makeshift tent," put in Rusty.

"We don't use our grain binder anymore since we bought a new combine to harvest the oats and soybeans," replied Bruce.

The horses were munching on grass near the oak and walnut trees. Chester and Rusty jumped on their mounts and were off in a cloud of dust. They trotted back home and started packing for the camping trip. They had bought a gallon of root beer, jam, buns, wieners, marshmallows, and candy at the general store. They packed some clothes and waited for Sam and Bruce.

They heard hoof beats and saw the two cousins come riding into the Wampuch farmyard with their packs. They wanted to get set up before dark, so they headed out towards the valley. Fred opened the fence gate, and they almost rode over some Plymouth-barred rock chickens that were on the path. It was a couple of hours before sunset when the teenagers crossed the green pasture and entered the woods. The Black Angus cattle were resting, and western meadowlarks were prancing around.

The four riders were walking the horses down an old road on a bluff that had been used for logging in the past. All was peaceful and quiet, and then suddenly, a rifle slug smashed off a rock with a loud zinging report a few yards in front of the riders. An echo followed it, and the boys halted their horses.

The four riders dismounted and spent a few minutes to look over the woods and valley below. Seeing nothing, they went on down the trail.

"I wonder who fired that shot?" asked Rusty.

"It could be a stray shot," said Bruce.

They soon reached the bottom where the trail branched off into two separate trails. Two riders were sighted coming out of a clump of trees.

"I know them," said Rusty.

The two groups halted in front of each other.

"Did you fire a shot a few minutes ago?" he asked.

"Yeah, we were out fox hunting, and we saw you guys coming down the trail, so I thought I'd scare the pants off you, and I fired the shot," said Kells, who was a neighbor.

"It was some scare all right. Did you see any fox yet?" asked Sammy.

"Only one, but it got away," replied Kells.

They exchanged a few more words, and the parties moved out in separate directions. Rusty's group turned left in the valley. A dry creek bed ran along the green valley with bluffs on both sides with oak, elm, pine, cedar, and fir trees.

The grass was high with more cattle in sight and a few chipmunks and woodchucks among the rocks along the cliff. After rounding a couple of bends, they came upon the swimming hole and unpacked their gear and tethered the horses. It was nearing dusk when the boys tied together the three canvasses with prison-made baler twine from Stillwater and made a three-sided tent.

The youths built a campfire from a pile of dead wood, twigs, and branches. They got a great blaze going, second only to the homecoming bonfires that schools have in the autumn. Since it was under an oak tree, it did not burn down. An evergreen tree would not have survived the heat.

"Let's get out the wieners and pop," said Chester.

The boys sat down with their legs crossed just like four Indian chiefs. They talked of old times when they were in grade school. They were having fun in the wilderness.

"Remember when we were in the woods behind the country schoolhouse and used an ax to chop down a few trees?" asked Rusty, while putting mustard on his wiener.

"Yeah, it was on a neighbor's farm, and he got mad at us boys who did it," said Chester.

They remembered the red brick school, the white frame eight-sided town hall, and the creamery.

"The wooden general store was built in the 1850's," said Rusty, while he roasted marshmallows.

"Remember when we used to stop there after school on our bikes and see the two old clerks playing cards!" addedSam.

"And the time when we got chased out of the haymow in the barn next to the store when they thought we were smoking cigarettes," commented Chester. He grabbed a wiener.

The foursome was having a superb time. After the late supper, they sat around the campfire and put a piece of wood on whenever the blaze died down. The horses were munching on the grass. Sometimes a loon or a fox cried out, among other strange noises. It seemed like a virgin wilderness.

"Did you hear the latest news?" asked Bruce.

"No, tell us," put in Sam, while drinking root beer.

"There is an Indian cop in Rushford and a Mexican bartender in Stockton. Well, if you go to Rushford, you get an arrow in your ass, and if you visit Stockton, you get a knife in your back," stated Bruce.

They laughed heartily.

"You better not let an Indian or a greaser hear you say that," warned Chester. He added a branch to the campfire.

The stars were out, and the moon was high when they rolled out their bedrolls. The boys retired inside the makeshift tent. They were not used to sleeping on the ground and were restless. Maybe it was because of the odd noises they heard in the woods. A superb sunrise welcomed them the next morning.

The gray gloom was turning to the golden glory of a new day. The cries of wild animals and birds were heard during the night. Rusty and Chester cut firewood, while Sam and Bruce did other camp chores. After heating up hot chocolate, oatmeal, toast, and jelly, they did some hiking and exploring on foot. Rusty found a stone that had been used by an Indian as a war club. It had markings in the center.

"I wonder what tribe this belonged to?" he asked.

"Maybe the Sioux," replied Chester. "They once roamed this area and had the second largest population of any tribe."

"The Iowas and Winnebagos may of been here also," added Rusty. "I know the Apaches had the most Indians."

The latter took out his hunting knife and carved his initials and date into a sandstone boulder, R.W.-- July 24, 1954. "I will return here when I am an old man and look at it."

Rusty and Chester hiked back to the campsite to find Sam and Bruce in the water.

"The water is perfect; come in!" said Sam.

The small pool was too shallow to dive into, so the boys would sit on a tree root and slide into the water. They had fun splashing around in their swimming trunks while taking turns being in the water and getting a suntan on the grass.

"You are lucky having a pool on your farm," said Chester.

"We are really having a good time!" said Sam.

"We have to enjoy ourselves now because think of where we will be in two months," said Bruce while adding sun lotion.

"Yeah, we will be in school," replied Sam.

The teenagers put saddles and bridles on the horses and paired off and chased each other through the forest and over a bluff on horseback.

They galloped up and down the trails and over a long green meadow. Rusty was daring as he barely missed tree limbs. He was riding with Chester, and they could have been compared to a Roy Rogers or a Gene Autry movie on the silver screen. That night, they made another campfire.

"It was a good thing that the oats and hay crops were harvested, otherwise our folks would have needed us at home to help," said the oldest teenager, Bruce.

"Work always comes before play for farmers," said Chester.

"A farmer is his own boss since he can take time off from work anytime and sleep under a tree or go to town and get a belly full of beer," observed Sam, the youngest.

"He would not get his work done that way," added Chester.

Carrol P. Peterson

"I wonder which star up there is the North Star?" asked Rusty while looking up at a dark void.

"You find the Big Dipper first; then look in a straight line from the tip and locate the North Star," stated Chester, the second oldest in the group.

The teenagers stayed up late again telling jokes. Rusty and Sam were great at storytelling.

As the coals died down, the youths called it a day and got out their sleeping bags and crawled in to sleep.

The next day, they did more scouting around and espied two deer. After a dip in the pool, they took down the tent and cleaned the area. They jumped over gullies on the way back to the barnyard on the horses. They had returned to civilization. Cindy was happy to see them again. Bruce went home while the others unpacked and did chores. Little blonde Cindy was playing outside in her orange shorts and shirt.

A couple of days later, the foursome got together again and motored over to a stream called Rush Creek.

"I know a good place to swim!" said Rusty. He found a place with a sandy beach and no people.

They spent time on the beach and in the water relaxing. Later, they hiked along the shore a long ways. Some fishermen were trying their luck downstream.

Rusty broke the silence. "We got fishing poles in the car, so let's try our luck!"

"That is the best idea I heard all day," said Chester.

Each grabbed a pole, line, hooks, and sinkers. They then dug for worms with a manure fork. The foursome spread out along Rush Creek and spent a couple of hours hauling in fish. They caught trout, suckers, and chubs, counting ten fish in all. The boys had a great time on that lazy, hazy, summer day.

That night, they became couch potatoes watching the black and white TV set. It was a Philco model.

Summer Mirage

"I like it when there is plenty of action with fighting and hard riding!" said Bruce. "Gunsmoke" was on with Marshall Matt Dillon in charge at Dodge City, Kansas.

"I bet that show lasts longer on television than all the other westerns," said Chester.

They watched intently as the human drama and action unfolded before them on the twenty-one inch TV screen as eight outlaws kissed the dust and went on one-way vacation trips to Boothill.

Later, the boys sat around a table to play "500" at cards with Rusty and Chester against Sam and Bruce. Hilda, the queen of the house, brought in popcorn and soda pop for them.

"We will have to do the same thing next summer," said Sam.

"I will drink to that!" agreed Chester.

"We should stay longer in the valley next time," added Rusty while sipping on his Seven-Up drink.

After a few games, Bruce left to go home. They had made plans for a hayride at Bruce Thompson's farm the next night.

Little Cindy joined the trio looking at books and magazines. Being cheerful, she asked, "What are you reading, Chester?"

"I am looking at Field and Stream. Are you going to school soon?" he asked her.

"Sure, and I can already read!"

Cindy read from a book, Black Beauty. Chester took a photo of her reading.

Hours later, the boys rose with the first rays of the sun. They felt young and fresh and ready for the good time expected ahead. In the barn they fed the calves milk from small pails, and then they carried corn and oats to the chickens.

Fred was driving a red Farmall tractor with a mower to cut weeds. Tim Wampuch, the farm owner, was loading manure with a pitchfork at the back of the barn. He wiped the sweat from his face.

"You can't hardly get a man to work on a farm nowadays," said Rusty. He took off his straw hat and looked at it.

"Who wants to work and sweat on a stinking farm?" said Chester.

He joined the two brothers in riding over to the farm of Bruce. They found him in the barn doing the milking. He had a good setup for dairying with two long rows of stanchions for the cows to stand in. Four calf pens were along the wall on one side of the barn. A gold-colored calendar with big red letters that read, "Rushford State Bank," was on the barn wall.

"Good evening," said Chester to the handsome male milker.

"Howdy. How long will you be staying at Rusty's farm?"

"A day or two longer."

"Don't stand too close to that black cow because she can send you flying like an airplane if she kicks you," warned Bruce.

They watched Bruce finish his chores; then all walked to the apple orchard and ate some red apples. Later, Bruce got all dressed up fine and dandy, putting on a new pair of Levis trousers and a blue corduroy shirt. Standing in front of a big mirror, he combed his hair, putting in a big wave with a pocket comb. Bruce had brown hair, just like Chester's, while Sam and his brother Rusty, had red hair.

"You are all set for the girls now," commented Sam.

"Don't get funny," replied Bruce with a little grin.

Soon, the neighbor youths began to arrive.

Chapter Nine

Nice cars filled the yard while an auburn-haired lady emerged from a tan-colored Hudson car and walked towards Chester. He and Tamra Hunt were both in green shirts and blue Levis.

"What have you been doing lately, Tamra?" Chester asked.

"Besides cooking, house chores, and some tractor driving, I am reading a book," she replied. "It is a good story about a girl who goes to Arizona after the First World War, and she keeps teasing the men who are all chasing her."

"I know that story; it is A Code of the West by Zane Grey," said Chester. "A superb novel."

They started off on the hayride. The youths settled back on the hay in the wagon and sang a few songs like, "Home on the Range," and "Oh, Susanna." The weather was pleasant on that August night. A small blue Ford tractor pulled them along a gravel road; there were ten passengers.

After dusk, Bruce had his arm around a pretty brunette, Estelle Gill. Rusty was with Molly Olson, a brown-haired, cute girl in blue jeans. Sam was talking to a neighbor. Tamra was close to Chester, her hair in his face.

"I suppose you do this every weekend," said Chester.

"With whom? I have been waiting for you to call me up for a date," replied Tamra.

That statement surprised Chester, and he had no answer. Maybe he didn't know what he had been missing.

Tamra pulled the blanket over her partner. They were in that position when the hayride stopped at the Wyattville store. Everyone entered the building for refreshments.

The genial old clerk made a few wise cracks, as usual. Later, they all returned home.

The next day, the friends played baseball. One person pitched while the others did the fielding. They had been on a baseball diamond a lot lately, and Chester could throw a curve, a fastball, and a change-up. He struck out the side in one inning. Rusty hit the longest ball of the day and was proud. They soon tired, and Bruce went home to his farm.

Chester and Rusty settled down to a game of checkers, then to a game of Parcheesi. As the guest was shaking the dice, Ole drove into the yard, and Chester's sojourn at the farm of Sam and Rusty Wampuch ended.

"Sorry you have to leave so soon," said Rusty.

"We will have happy times when you come to visit me," replied his pal.

"Goodbye," uttered Chester, as he grabbed a suitcase and walked down the stairs.

Maybe the number of days Chester was a guest was at the right length. Sometimes when friends stay together too long, differences and arguments develop. But then, these four youths had a unique friendship that could be everlasting.

Chester arrived home just in time to clean a chicken coop. He disliked that job the worst. It took two days to do it since there were four loads of manure to haul out with a lot of tiring walking inside the old, wood-frame building.

His agriculture teacher in high school, who had gone broke farming himself, had said that chicken shit was the best manure for the soil. Ole, Louie, and Chester walked back and forth, carrying the hen manure in forks and shovels to the manure spreader parked next to a door.

"Did you have fun during your stay at Rusty's farm?" asked Louie during a pause from working.

"Yep, and the weather was perfect for the camping, riding horseback, swimming, fishing, and exploring," said Chester.

"Did you find anything?" queried Ole.

"Yeah, Rusty found an Indian war club," Chester said.

They soon got a load on the John Deere manure spreader and took a rest. There were a few sick looking chickens staggering around looking as though they had drunk beer instead of water. Ole grabbed each and put them between his legs to get a good hold and stretched their necks. He then heaved the dead hens into the spreader and later hawks would have a feast on the carcasses. Louie hauled out the manure.

"Bernie Baker is in the jailhouse," said Ole. "He was on a drunk, and Les wanted him caged for a while because he can't spend his money behind bars."

"That dumb bastard!" replied Chester.

It was the week before school was to start in September, and it was Rusty's turn to visit his friend. Chester was resting under a pine tree after the noon dinner when he heard a horse come galloping on the gravel road. It was Rusty on his bay, Tony.

"Howdy, cowboy," greeted Chester.

"Howdy, pardner," he replied, as though he had seen too many western movies. "What were you and Tamra doing under that blanket on that hayride?" queried Rusty.

"You don't know, do you? Come to the house for a root beer; you may be thirsty after that ride."

"It got dusty after cars passed me on the gravel road," said Rusty.

The two pals loaded a pup tent and camping supplies into Chester's second car, a 1937 black Plymouth sedan, and took the road to Rush Creek. He floored the gas petal, and the car reached fifty-five miles per hour. They left the main road and went over some fields to a lane at the edge of a cornfield and parked the family car.

They grabbed the camping gear and fishing poles and walked down a bluff path among oak, elm, hickory, apple, and fir trees. Below them the creek was flowing like a long ribbon meandering to a distant place.

"I would not want to fall off the side of this bluff," said Rusty.

"Especially when we are carrying a load on our backs," added Chester.

They set up the tent upon reaching the shore and placed the supplies inside. After a rest on the bank, the boys entered the creek for a swim, and each did a jellyfish float and the dog paddle.

"I hope to be a Navy Frogman some day," said Rusty. He had just seen the movie, The Frogmen, starring Richard Widmark.

"There are fish here, but let's walk downstream and look before we wet our lines," suggested Rusty.

They fished at several places and pulled in trout, suckers, and chubs. A mud turtle and beaver dam were seen there in the valley.

At dusk in the golden, western sky, they had a fish fry and marshmallow roast on the creek bank. Rusty went to get two bottles of soda pop that had been kept cold in the creek. The meal was great there in the outdoors where for centuries Indians had been traversing the area.

Rusty and Chester sat around the blazing campfire and talked about the old radio programs of "Straight Arrow," "Tom Mix," "Mark Trail," "Bobby Benson and the B Bar B Ranch," and "The Lone Ranger."

Each had been a half-hour adventure program on radio just before television had become popular. All were in comic books also.

"Are you going out for any sports in the fall?" asked Chester.

"I am trying out for football. What about you?" Rusty asked.

"I guess I will be too busy with farm chores," replied Chester.

"I hope the cattle don't come down here while we are camping," said Rusty. "I wonder if a big bull roams around here?"

"A bull with horns can be as dangerous as a pack of wolves," said Chester.

They stared at the hot coals in the campfire. Chester thought he saw Tamra's face in the amber glow.

A Jersey cow mooed off in the distance, and an owl hooted, winking his huge eyes. They roasted more marshmallows by using sharp sticks and then sat down like a couple of Indian chiefs.

"How about going hunting up north in November?" asked the red head.

"Yeah, we can try our luck for deer near the border town of Warroad or Bemidji," replied Chester.

"I will ask Sam and my cousin Bruce if they want to come along."

"Good, the more the merrier," said Chester.

The campfire died down as they entered the tent and closed the flaps for the night. It got chilly as the hours passed by.

At dawn, there was moisture on the lining of the tent. Peering out of the flaps, they could see that the sky was cloudy. Then came the loud bellowing of a big Jersey bull. It started towards the boys at a trot.

"Holy Moses, let's get out of here!" exhorted Chester.

They rushed out of the tent and went into the creek as the bull with horns trotted up to the creek and stared at the boys.

"Get going, you mad bull," said Rusty.

After a few minutes, the bull went back to his herd of cattle in the pasture.

"It was a good thing we woke up early or that bull might have been pushing the tent down of top of us," said Chester.

"Let's explore in the other direction this morning," Rusty suggested; he always had good ideas.

They carried hunting knives while crossing hills and came upon an old abandoned farm, which had not been occupied since 1937.

"This is a ghost farm!" said Chester.

The wood-frame buildings were gray and in poor condition. A strong wind would probably level the place. The structures had been standing for about one hundred years. The boys walked to the house and were surprised to see pigs inside, making themselves at home. They were brown, Duroc hogs nosing around in empty rooms.

"It looks like a farmer is renting this farm, but nobody is living here now," said Chester.

Then the rain began to fall as they raced for cover at a barn. There were more cattle by the pond. As they huddled in the barn, Chester had some questions.

How many families and babies had grown up there? What human drama there must have been. Had there been love, violence, and accidents?

"I would like to know the answers too," said Rusty. "This place spooks me," he added.

They waited until the rain ended.

"Let's hit the road," said Chester.

Two fish were on the lines when the boys returned to Rush Creek.

"There will be fish in a pan for supper tonight," said Rusty.

They entered the water for a swim first and did not mind it being a little muddy from the rain.

Later, Rusty cleaned the fish, and his pal did the frying. The boys had bread, jam, peaches, and carrots. Before dark, the tent was set up on the other side of the creek where the bull could not show his ugly head. Then they went out with a hatchet to gather firewood for the next day.

Later, the boys sat around the warm campfire and played poker at cards. They added branches and twigs to the blaze between games. When the moon came out, they went to sleep.

At dawn, the boys were up as the golden sunbeams filtered through the trees on the bluff. Steam was on the creek since the temperature of the water and air differed.

After breakfast, the two-some put their things in order and took down the tent. They tidied up the campsite and then started up the bluff path. It was a laborious hike carrying loads up the hill. They reached the summit, and Rusty looked surprised when he neared the black Plymouth car. He took off his hat.

"Holy smokes, come quick. Look at the car," he stated with emotion. "There are two flat tires, and the doors are all wired shut to the steering wheel."

"Who could have done such a thing?" queried Chester as he gazed in amazement.

They unraveled the wires, which were on tight and found pliers in the trunk. After removing the wires from the door handles, they jacked up the car to change a tire.

"I bet it was that farmer with a Roman nose and fat wife. We knocked down some of his corn stalks when we drove in here, so he must have gotten mad," said Chester.

"There is a farm just over yonder, so let's start to roll this other flat tire over there, and maybe that farmer will let us use a telephone," said Rusty.

That proved to be a big job because of the rain. The tire got muddy, along with the boys' hands and clothes. A mist was falling as they reached the farmhouse; the old bachelor let them use a phone.

Chester dialed home, and Lucy came on the line.

"I will send Ole over to pick you boys up," she said.

They thanked John and waited. Things finally worked out all right, and Rusty and his friends got the car out of the muddy field. They cleaned up and ate supper.

Later, the friends strolled over to a big pine tree; the sky was hazy with insects in the air. The sun was setting over the forest with a gold and scarlet sunset.

Rusty mounted his sturdy bay saying, "Let's ride, Tony; it's time to go home." He neck reined Tony around and went into that sunset, down into the driveway, just as Gene Autry had frequently done in the movies.

"Take it easy," he called out.

"Don't run Tony too hard on the gravel road," Chester called back.

As Rusty turned the corner, he lifted his brown cowboy hat and waved it. Chester waved his white hat in a return salute. They would never forget that summer vacation when the old General, Ike, was in the White House. It was still a few days before school would begin.

Louie and his older brother, Chester, sat down in the west room for a game of Monopoly. They lived in the two-story, white wood-frame Victorian-style house that was about a hundred years old.

Louie had wavy, brown hair and was already a hit with the girls in school. He was in his early teens."Do you want to play a game of Parcheesi after this?" he asked.

"Yeah, that is a good game imported from India," replied Chester.

They were seated at a card table.

"Did you see any deer while you were camping with Rusty?"

"I only saw two when the four of us were in the Wampuch Valley camping," replied Chester. "I plan on going deer hunting up north in November with Rusty, Sam, and Bruce."

"I am going hunting in this area in the fall," said Louie.

Chester won the game of Monopoly, and then they got out a Parcheesi set. They shook the dice to see who would move first. Louie won the shake and later the game after capturing four red pieces.

Then Chester got a bright idea. "Let's drive up to the Minnesota State Fair? It ends on Labor Day!"

"Sure, let's get going!" said Louie.

They hopped into the blue 1952 Chevy, swung onto Highway 61, and drove up by the Mississippi River. They stopped at Red Wing for lunch. Later, the boys ran into heavy traffic as they entered the fair area.

They parked by the entrance gate and locked up the Chevy. They were at the greatest State Fair in the world, but the Texans might have argued that. Louie and Chester paused at the Bonanza lunch stand for a drink. A radio on a loud speaker was playing the number-one song in the nation, "Volare," by Dean Martin.

They went to the barns to see the cattle, sheep, hogs, chickens, and horses. Les Grey had said he could spend a whole day in the hog barn alone. The boys next viewed the exhibits of vegetables, fruits, honey, and products raised by farmers. The brothers strolled out to the midway and rode on a Ferris wheel.

When it halted at the top, Chester said, "Did you know that only a needle holds us up here?"

"It must be a big, fat needle," replied Louie.

They later attended a colored show, sitting in the second row. A comedian came on the stage, followed by scantly clad female dancers. The band was too loud with its music.

That night, they attended the Western horse show in the concrete block hippodrome or coliseum. A parade of cowboys and cowgirls in their colorful attire started the program. Then came a rodeo with bucking horses and calf roping with clowns.

A team of small horses came galloping into the arena, pulling a wagon. Then came a majestic team of Clydesdales in front of the Budweiser beer wagon. What big horses!

"Did you get enough milk to drink at the Dairy Association bar?" asked Louie. "I drank eight cups!"

"I had ten cups for a dime," said Chester.

That was a white concession stand where one was allowed to drink all he could for a dime. That night they slept in the car.

The next day, the boys visited Machinery Hill to see the colorful tractors and implements. In the dairy building, they espied the lovely girl, Princess Kay of the Milky Way, a farm girl. Ten regional princesses modeled close to a sculptor, who made a model of each girl out of butter.

To top off the evening, Louie and Chester attended a show in the grandstand to see comedian Bob Hope. They left the big fairgrounds after the fireworks spectacle for the one-hundred-mile journey home. Taking a different route, they stopped at a Golden Fox restaurant north of Rochester. There were tall cornfields in all directions.

"What did you think of the cowgirls at the horse show?"

"They were dressed up pretty in their colorful clothes, and their saddles were expensive," replied Chester.

It was late at night when the brothers pulled into the farm driveway. The black and white English shepherd, Adolf, greeted them. It felt good to hit the sack after walking for two days at the big fair.

Chapter Ten

Lester Grey had been to town and was returning home with his hired man, Bernie Baker. The latter was still drunk as they halted at the garage. Les went to the barn to start chores, and Bernie staggered to the house to sober up. He sat at the table with his head bowed, eyes closed, his lower lip protruding, and his face red. He mumbled some words.

Alice Grey poured Bernie a hot cup of coffee saying, "Have some coffee; you need it."

"Huh? Oh, yeah." He opened his bloodshot eyes and drank.

He then rose and went to lie down on a davenport. Alice turned on the TV set to hear a news report. Soon, Les came for supper. The coffee sobered Bernie up, and he joined the couple in eating.

"We are going over to Ole's farm soon to fill silo," said Lester. "Can you help with the milking tonight?"

"Oh, hell yes, I'm okay," replied Bernie.

"Chester will help fill silo when he returns from school, so then I can leave," added Les with a mouthful of food.

The men walked out to the red-painted barn.

Bernie felt better after having fresh air and some work. He moved around faster and was sweating. As he was locking up the cows, one of them stepped on his foot.

"Owww, you rotten son-of-a-bitch!" he yelled as he twisted the cow's tail, breaking it, and he kicked her in the belly.

Summer Mirage

The dumb animal belched and farted. Bernie then grabbed a barn broom and swept the floor.

A black and white Holstein swung her tail and hit Bernie across his eye, stinging his face, causing him to have tears falling.

"Jesus balls, you evil bastard," he uttered. Bernie was obnoxious while picking up a leather strap, and he whipped the heifer until he was all played out. The animal heaved and puked as Les shook his head while noticing his strange and agitated hired man. Les put the radio on to old-time music.

The Whoopee John band played the "Minnesota Polka." Then the Blue Banners played Harry Truman's favorite tune, the "Missouri Waltz."

They finished milking, and Bernie climbed a hay chute to heave down some hay. There was not much grass left in the pasture. Les carried a block of salt outside and put it in a feed bunk. When the cows had the hay eaten, the men let them outside, and Bernie swept the floor.

That evening, they had supper on the picnic table. Alice brought banana splits with chocolate topping out there on the front lawn. Les was about fourteen years older than his wife, Alice.

"You can take the John Deere tractor over to Ole's farm tomorrow, and I will take the pickup," said the boss. "Where were you the other night?"

"At the Crystal Palace saloon in La Crosse, and I saw Sally there, and we danced until I was too drunk to stand up," replied Bernie.

Alice carried out glasses of wine.

"I am going in the house and read The Winona Daily News now," said Lester.

Later, Bernie followed, and he read the comic pages while laughing. Then it grew quiet in the Grey house as they went to bed.

At daybreak, the men rose early to do barn chores. After breakfast, Bernie mounted the tractor and with a forage wagon hitched behind, headed out onto the county road. He stripped the gears and spun the wheels upon starting out.

As he rounded the first curve, he drove too close to the ditch, and the large wagon toppled over. "God, damn it, of all the luck!" roared Bernie.

Les saw the accident, and he took another tractor and sped over to the site.

"Christ almighty, why don't you watch where you are going? Don't be so damn dumb and reckless!" added the boss.

"It's not my fault that a county engineer planned the ditch too steep," replied Bernie.

"That is a good excuse; well, let's get the damn wagon upright," said Lester.

Les tied two ropes onto the wagon in the ditch and hitched them to the other tractor. That worked, and they got the hay wagon back onto the road.

Bernie came to a hill and put the clutch into neutral, and the tractor and wagon coasted downhill. He finally arrived at the Ole Borseth farm, and Lester was in his Dodge green pickup waiting. It was a bright September day.

"Climb up the silo, Bernie, and we will send up the pipe," said Les.

They hooked one end of the rope to the pipe, near the center, and the other end to the tractor. Ole drove the tractor while Les guided the pipe up the silo. Bernie was at the top of the concrete block silo, about sixty feet high.

"Watch your footing; I don't want to clean up your mess if you fall down!" Les shouted upwards.

"Don't worry about me!" Bernie called down. He put a finger on the side of his odd nose and blew a wad of yellow snot onto the machine below. A gust of wind blew the cap off his head.

As the pipe came up, Bernie guided the spout into the silo door. Les assisted as the two farm owners tied the rope into place down below, and they backed the blower up by hand. Now they were all set to chop corn silage for the cattle's winter feed.

It was noontime, so the men walked to the house for dinner. Lucy was putting food on the table, while Ole always put more dirt on the towel than in the sink. He never used enough soap and was always in a hurry to eat.

"I don't know what you got in the oven, but it smells good," said Les while looking at Lucy in her orange dress.

"It is apple pie," replied the housewife.

"What time does Chester get home?" he asked.

"He gets off the bus by four o'clock."

"I aim to return home to start chores around that time," added Les.

"Did you go to Belmont's funeral?"

"Yep, I did and even Slim Red was there," replied Ole.

"I bet he did not shed a tear," said Lester.

"Belmont's wife, Shirley, didn't either; nobody did."

Soon, Ole went out with the tractor, chopper, and green wagon to load up corn silage. Bernie took the John Deere and an empty wagon and drove out to meet Ole. Soon, Bernie returned to the silo with a full load, and Les started the blower with a crank. The two men pitched off the corn silage from the back of the wagon with pitchforks.

Between loads, Les listened to a baseball game on a radio in the barn while sitting near the wall. A white cat was next to a milk pan drinking along with Adolf, the dog.

A few miles away, Tamra Hunt and Chester Borseth were on the way out of the high school.

"Call me at supper time," she said.

"I will call you from the black rotary phone in the milk house," he replied.

"Don't forget!" demanded the auburn-haired beauty.

The handsome couple walked to different school buses since they lived on different routes.

The bus ride home for Chester was about nine miles because the driver, a veteran of World War One, did not drive directly to the Borseth farm. Sometimes, Chester drove the Chevy to school and arrived home sooner after school let out. His teacher, Gordy, had said that the shortest distance between two points was a straight line. Chester chatted with students on the bus.

Carrol P. Peterson

A road grader was smoothing out the gravel down the road, making the county road easier to drive on. Chester entered his house, glanced at the mail, and changed from school clothes to work clothes. Then he went outside to help unload silage from a wagon. He espied Bernie smoking an Old Gold cigarette and taking a leak on the ground. He wore a straw hat.

"How was school?" he asked. "Did you learn anything today?"

"Yeah, I learned that there were American presidents born in every month of the year except June, and that none died in May, and James Buchanan was the only bachelor president."

"By jinks, I wish I was as smart as you!" replied Bernie.

Les left in his green Dodge pickup truck for home. Bernie, Ole, and Chester continued filling silo.

"Who won the baseball game today?" asked Chester.

"The Cardinals did," responded Bernie.

"To error is human," commented the teenager on the Braves' loss and mistakes on the field.

Chester took the jack off the wagon and drove out into the field for another load. Bernie pulled the rope that idled the motor on the blower. Thus they worked until they got seven loads of corn silage into the silo that day.

Chester called up his girlfriend from the phone in the milk house. As he was dialing the four digits, calves were bellowing for hay or milk in the barn next door. He shut the swinging door to close out the noise. He was standing next to the big stainless steel Zero bulk milk tank.

"What are you doing today?" asked Tamra.

"We have been filling silo," said Chester.

"With what, ice cream?" she asked jokingly.

"Ha, ha, that is not a bad idea since it would not melt much in the winter, but today we put in corn silage."

"How about going to a party at the roller skating rink?"

"I will pick you up at eight," said Chester. He returned to the barn to finish the chores.

Later, Chester took his Chevy to pick up Tamra. Soon, he was wheeling past the windbreak of fir and pine trees and saw roses in bloom around her house. An English shepherd dog looked him over as he neared the front door. Lamps were on in the house; they could be seen through the windows.

Tamra came out wearing a blue sweater and brown slacks. She was sixteen, slim, and strong.

"Right on time as usual," she said smartly.

"What time does the skating party start?" asked Chester.

"It will start for us when we arrive there. Do you still drive the 1937 Plymouth?"

"Sometimes, since there is nostalgia with it," said Chester.

"We can stop at the Wyattville store and buy some things," she suggested.

They soon arrived and saw some cars parked. A poster on a wall told of a wedding dance that night. The Whoopee John band was coming to play old-time music.

Tamra bought household articles, and Chester got hunting supplies and an orange cap. Then they left for Winona. The blacktop road went down the big valley below. They passed by Lake Winona and wooded bluffs. On one bluff stood the local landmark called "Sugarloaf."

The couple parked next to the National Guard Armory where the roller skating was in progress. They saw a young crowd of teens while they were putting skating shoes on. Tamra talked to some girls, and Chester bought a few candy bars.

"Everybody can skate now," said the announcer, and everyone rolled out onto the wooden floor. Later, couples only skated, and Chester and Tamra went around the circle hand in hand and arms around each other's waists. The tune, "Melody of Love," was on the phonograph, and the colored lights were low and dim. They were good at skating.

"Let's leave early and stop at the dance," said Tamra.

"That's a good idea," replied Chester.

She always had good ideas, like Rusty.

She said goodbye to a few girls while a man was showing off by lying on the floor and shouting loudly. A big orange moon was hanging over the Sugarloaf bluff. Soon, they were back at the hamlet of Wyattville for the dance.

Carrol P. Peterson

The bar was so crowded that one could barely move about. The band was playing the fast-paced "Minnesota Polka," and all laughed at a fat couple bouncing around like two walruses.

Chester paid the admission, and they danced to the "Blue Danube Waltz." They danced close together in a romantic setting. They stayed on the floor for a fox trot and then the "Milwaukee Waltz."

After sitting down for a while, they entered the bar to see Bernie at a stool drinking Coca-Cola. Chester tapped him on the shoulder, and he was surprised.

"Are you two enjoying the fun?" he asked.

"So far, so good!" replied Chester.

Bernie continued to talk to a man nearby. The couple returned to the dance floor and saw a loudmouth who yelled, "Whoppee" occasionally.

Tamra's parents did not care what time their pretty daughter returned home because they knew she was old enough to think for herself. They left the dance and returned to the Hunt farm by midnight. The teenagers walked to the door and embraced and kissed good night. The silvery glow of the moon highlighted her auburn hair, and some of Tamra's lipstick stayed on Chester's cheek. They had not kissed since the hayrides. He noticed her perfume that smelled like peaches.

"See you at school," she murmured while the door edged shut.

"See you, peaches," he answered.

The stars were out as he thought that his relationship with Tamra would endure, and he knew that she was a thoroughbred person.

Some weeks passed by, and it was corn-picking time. The leaves on the hardwood trees of oak, walnut, ash, and birch were turning gold, scarlet, purple, and brown in an array of bright colors. It was October in the upper Midwest, and the pumpkins were ripening. There were nights of frost.

Chapter Eleven

One day as Chester got off the school bus, Les was on a tractor picking corn in the field. He had a two-row picker on a John Deere tractor. As Chester walked to the 19th century corncrib, he saw Ole unloading a wagon full of ear corn. A jack raised the front up, and the golden ears of husked corn were sliding out the rear while Ole pushed them with a shovel.

When the wagon was empty, Chester hauled it back to the field to pick up another load. He stopped at the site where Les was located just as he got a load of corn. An Old Gold cigarette hung from Les' mouth, and he lighted it with the push-button lighter on the tractor. They exchanged wagons.

"You back from school already?" asked Lester.

"Yep, I just got home," replied Chester.

Les was wearing an extra layer of clothes as the autumn days were chilly even when the sun was shining.

"I plan on stopping picking corn at six o'clock," said Les. A brisk wind picked up as Les asked the temperature.

"It is forty-five degrees Fahrenheit," said Chester.

Stratus clouds had formed in the sky. When the wooden corncrib got filled, Ole and his son put up another one, which consisted of two snow fences in a circle, one on top of another.

Chester backed the tractor and wagon with corn up to the red Diedrich model elevator. He pulled on the cord to get the motor started.

They unloaded a few more loads that day before Les quit picking in the field. Lucy had a good chicken supper ready in the warm kitchen, with beets, potatoes, fresh bread, and pumpkin pie with whipped cream.

"You will have to trap those pocket gophers soon, Chester," said Les, while filling his plate with food.

"Yeah, I noticed the black mounds in the field," Chester replied.

"It seems like they dig in the spring; then they're lazy during the summer. Then they dig again before the snow flies," said Ole.

"I got nine traps and will set them up this weekend," said Chester.

Lucy brought more coffee and milk.

"Has there been any more excitement on the Town Board?" queried Lester.

"It has been quiet since the Belmont and Slim Red fracas," answered Ole. He always drank cold water at mealtime.

"How about more chicken or tomatoes?" asked Lucy.

"Sure, I am a working man and a big eater too," said Les. He was outspoken and always said what he thought.

In that way he was like Matt Dillon on TV's "Gunsmoke," and like Harry "give them hell" Truman, who had occupied the White House. Those men always said exactly what they meant, unlike many dumb fools walking with their heads down and not seeing where they were going.

The dog, Adolf, was lying in the corner by the house.

"I wonder what is the matter with the dog?" asked Louie, who had gotten off the school bus before supper.

"He might have eaten something that did not agree with him," said Ole. "I never enjoyed having a dog lick me because I never knew what he had been licking previous to that."

"How many days before you finish picking corn?" asked Ole.

"One more day, but I plan to start with my fall plowing in the morning and will send Bernie out here to finish with the cornfield," explained Les. He soon left.

After the meal, Louie and Chester looked at programs on the boob tube. Each came on TV with a singing entrance. "Tombstone Territory" then "Stories of the Century," starring the tall and sturdy Jim Davis as a western railroad detective chasing Jesse James, played by Lee Van Cleef.

After five men had been bored by lead slugs, the boys headed for the barn to do the chores. Later, they looked at the Farm Journal magazine. Ole and Lucy watched the "Lawrence Welk" show.

The next day, Chester drove Ole's new yellow-green Chevy to school. His first class was in agriculture with seven boys, all from farms. After the roll call, Gordy, the instructor, took them to his farm on the edge of town. He had a large flock of white and brown hens, and the chicken coop was neat and clean. Gordy was both a teacher and a farmer. The hens were clucking and drinking from fountains.

"I clean out the building every Saturday," said Gordy.

"We clean out our chicken coop two times a year," said his good student, Chester.

The group then walked to the football field where another class had planted a windbreak of Norway pines. The students dug a few holes in the ground to take soil samples. They heard quacking above as a flock of ducks flew by.

Later, there was the usual rush in the lunch line at school for a noon meal. The students acted like a pack of wild dogs gone hungry. As Chester was standing in line, Phillip, one of the dumbest boys in class, walked in front of him and cut into the line. Chester did not pay any attention just then, but just as they were to be served by the old ladies, he walked past Phillip when he was talking to a pal.

Phillip grabbed Chester by the waist and tried to pull him back, but Chester hung onto the table and retained his place in line. Some time later, they were eating next to each other.

"I will knock you down for that," said Phillip.

"You and whose army?" asked Chester.

The boy looked mean, but he continued eating.

When school let out, Chester walked with Tamra to the car parked next to the two-story brick schoolhouse built in 1906. She had on that peachy perfume again.

"It is about time you gave me a ride in your family's new car," she said.

They drove to the Borseth farm, and Tamra helped Lucy with the supper. It was a pleasant change having a young lady in the house. Chester helped with the corn harvest.

Bernie was still rough on the machinery, and he ran the tractor and picker as though they would last forever, never slowing down for the bumps.

He also stripped the gears and made noise. Chester then stopped with the "B" John Deere and wagon and waited for him to reach the end of a row with a load of corn. He thought Bernie Baker was quite a character with those bloodshot, bulging eyes, crooked nose, and an Old Gold cigarette hanging from his mouth.

"How's it going, Chester?" asked Les' hired man as he got off from his tractor.

"Okay, I guess," Chester replied nonchalantly.

"Did you go all the way with Tamra yet?"

"All what way?" said Chester.

"Ha, ha, ha," laughed Bernie like a hyena on the African plains.

They exchanged wagons, and the teenager took the full one home to unload.

Later at supper, Tamra and Lucy served a meal of ham and eggs, squash, and apple pie with ice cream.

"Gee, this is a real banquet!" spoke up Bernie.

"I have good help tonight with Tamra Hunt here," said Lucy.

"So I see," added Bernie as he looked Tamra over with his big, greedy eyes. "I finished the corn picking today."

"It is good to get it off the field before the snow flies," said Ole while he was filling his tank with food.

"We did have some snow flurries this month," said Chester.

"It did not amount to much though," commented Louie.

It was chilly outside, and the hearty meal warmed everyone up.

The men chatted about farming, the weather, and the neighbors. It was a different kind of conversation from that of some city folks sitting around a coffee table. Ole and Bernie did not give a damn about the world news, the goofy stock market, or the newest music records. If fifty people died on the highways over a holiday weekend, it was just fewer hungry faces for the lazy farmers to feed.

Chester went into the living room to read the newspaper. He soon followed the men outside, while Tamra helped with the dishes. After the chores were done, Chester changed clothes, and then he and Tamra took the road for Rushford. She steered the blue 1952 Chevy as they passed over the prairie. On a curve in the road stood a large deer in the ditch. It was still there when they were way down the road.

Then they entered a forest of white pine, balsam fir, and cedar trees. Off to the side lay Pine Creek, meandering down the valley. They drove through the valley and crossed the bridge over Rush Creek into town. Tamra parked by Hanson's Drug Store, and they bought a few articles. Later, they went to the Trojan Theater to see "Shane" with Alan Ladd; the movie was set in Wyoming. They both liked western movies. They later stopped at a drive-in eating place.

"How old are you?" asked Tamra.

"I am two years older than you," said Chester.

"What work do you plan on after high school?" she asked.

"I don't know, but maybe I will stay on the farm. What are your plans for after school?"

"I am not sure yet, but you can save your money so we can go together and share the experience," continued Tamra.

"That is a good idea; I will go and take a few courses and then after a year in college, I will know what I like best and major in that," said Chester.

"The first year is all general education courses anyway. I sent for a college catalog," she added.

They finished their cherry malts and left town with Chester driving.

"I heard that Les Grey's slave is an alcoholic," said his date.

"Ha, ha, he does work like a slave, but he earns good money and goes on a four-day drunk about every five months, and I don't know why Les tolerates it," said Chester. "I saw them argue once last autumn, and they shouted at each other."

"Bernie must have had some bad breaks in his past," said Tammy.

"He does not spend all of his money on alcoholic drinks and Old Gold cigarettes though because he gives some cash to his sister in Wisconsin," added Chester.

They drove along without talking for a spell, just listening to the music on the radio, including, "Lisbon Antigua," by Lex Baxter and "The Poor People of Paris" and "Canadian Sunset" by the Hugo Winteralter orchestra. Then Pat Boone sang "Love Letters in the Sand." Finally, Tamra reached her house.

"Goodnight," murmured the girl as she stepped out of the car.

"I wish you sweet dreams and goodnight," said Chester.

Before long, it was Thanksgiving morning, and Ole, Louie, and Chester did the work in the barn, picking eggs and feeding chickens while Lucy did the cooking. Then they all changed clothes and cleaned up because company was coming.

The boys were looking at a football game on television when Les, Alice, and Bernie drove into the yard. Lucy held a door open as they entered and left their coats in the bedroom. Ole passed out highballs of Sunny Brook whiskey mixed with Coca-Cola. Then the big feast began. On the table were milk, turkey, corn, potatoes, cranberries, homemade bread, and pumpkin pie.

"Did you get enough to eat yet?" asked Ole when they were on the dessert.

"I just started to fill my tank," replied Bernie.

"That was funny, Bernie!" said Louie with a mouthful of food.

Bernie did not drink anything while eating, but later sipped his coffee while smoking a cigarette. Ole had a drink of water with each mouthful. Maybe that was why he was fat, since he did not chew his food enough.

"Did you take out any hot women lately?" asked Louie.

"Hell, no. Les has kept me busy with farm work," said Bernie.

Ole and Les lay down to rest after the feast. The boys played ring toss, and even Bernie joined in on a game. Then all sat on easy chairs and looked at the holiday games of football on the black and white TV screen.

Summer Mirage

"I cannot see how anyone can be so stupid to pay hard-earned money to watch some big, ignorant brutes in uniforms push each other around on the ground," stated Ole.

"It's the clever announcers with their overstatements that suckers dumb fools into buying tickets," added Lester.

The men entered the kitchen to grab bottles of Bub's beer. A card table was set up for "500" at cards, and Bernie and Chester, two opposites, stood Les and his wife, Alice, in the game. They were all good players. After Bernie and Chester had won two of three games, Les stood up.

"Get your coats so we can go home; those cows don't get milked by themselves."

"They don't feed themselves either, since the pasture is all eaten up," added Bernie.

Surprisingly, the alcohol had not eaten up all of Bernie Baker's brains because at times he could exhibit a hint of intelligence. The Grey outfit took their leave while the others changed back into their work clothes.

Chester was soon in the barn doing the evening milking and handling two Surge units while Ole operated the other two. The fat man let loose a book-slamming fart while hanging a unit on a cow. The big bull in a pen boomed a loud cannon fart in a response. Nobody wanted to mess with him. Meanwhile, the cats were waiting for a pan of milk.

Later, Chester dressed for a late holiday supper at Tamra's house. He wondered what they were having for a meal. He drove over to the Hunt spread and parked in a grove of pines. Her mother came to the door to greet him.

"Come in; Tammy is in her bedroom getting ready, and I got a goose in the oven," said June.

"Thanks, the food smells good," replied Chester.

He entered the living room where the television was on. The program "I Got a Secret" with funny Henry Morgan, tall Bill Cullen, blonde Betsy Palmer, and Bess Myerson, a brunette and Miss America 1945, were the panelists, with Gary Moore as the host with his crewcut hair style. Tamra joined Chester on the couch.

"Have there been any interesting guests on the show yet?"

"I have not watched it long enough to find out," he replied.

They talked about the popular western programs.

"The good guys always win, and the hero rides off into the sunset," said Tamra. "The only thing the cowboy kisses is his horse," she observed.

"That is the way it happens on American TV and movies, but in many foreign films, the story has a sad ending, and the hero dies," commented Chester.

"You should be a drama critic," she said.

Tamra's father, Henry Hunt, with slightly graying hair, entered the house.

"How about a bottle of Seven-Up?" he asked.

"It sounds good, thanks," replied Chester.

Tamra rose to help June carry in the sweet potatoes, buns, cranberries, beets, rutabagas, nut bread, and goose meat.

"I am in the junior class play," said Tamra.

"What is the title of the play?" asked her pal.

"Hamlet, the greatest play ever written," said Tammy.

Tamra's mother may have looked a lot like her daughter thirty years earlier. She was still lovely to look at in her blue dress.

"We will have to see that stage play one night," said June.

"When does the play start?" asked Henry.

"In another week, and I have play practice tomorrow night," replied Tamra.

Her mother served cherry pie with ice cream.

Tamra brought out her chess set after the Thanksgiving meal. All the pieces and the board were made of onyx stone.

"It is a handsome set; where did you get it?" asked Chester.

"My folks bought it for me when they were on a vacation in Mexico last Christmas," she replied. "Do you play?"

"I have been playing for a year," he said.

Chester got the white pieces, while Tamra with her dark green pieces started checking Chester and forced his king into a corner. It was a corner of no return because soon he had to sacrifice his queen to avoid checkmate. She put her rooks and queen into good position and then on two smart moves, shifted her knights and got him in checkmate.

"I love the knights because they move with a lot of versatility," said Tammy.

"Yep, especially when you move them and you win," he said.

Tamra went to the refrigerator and got two bottles of Royal Crown Cola. It was cold enough without adding ice cubes.

"I have had enough chess for tonight. My eyes are tired, so when that happens I see the chess board, but not the right moves to play, and it's a paradox," explained Chester.

"I will see you later and goodnight to all," said Chester, while they said likewise in unison.

When he was driving home, Chester was thinking that chess was like a game of war, but with no injuries. It had been a happy day with plenty to eat.

Chapter Twelve

A week passed by, and it was the night of the play, Shakespeare's Hamlet, at the school auditorium. Tamra was playing the role of pretty Ophelia, and a ghost appeared in Act One; the ghost livened up the audience. Later, Ophelia drowned, and Tamra and the cast put on a good show. As the crowd filed out, Chester waited for her.

"How did you like it?" she asked.

"It was the greatest play I ever saw!" he replied. "It seemed so real during the sword fight when I could hear the clap and clang of the swords."

"Yeah, but they were not sharp," said Tamra.

They walked down the hall then towards the car in the rain and wind.

"I am glad I shut the car windows before the class play because it was cloudy out," said Chester.

They drove to the bowling alley to bowl a few games. He owned a purple plastic ball. Each player had a few errors in game one, but in the second they each ended with a double.

Chester bowled errorlessly with only one unconverted split in the last game and had a 203 score.

"That was fun bowling!" said the actress.

They stopped at the root beer drive-in for drinks. There were several girls waiting on cars; they were wearing Levis trousers and sweaters that did not match colors. It had stopped raining, and the sun was out. It was getting late when all drove home after the refreshments.

"Your car is dirty, and I can help you wash it," said Tamra.

"No, I will do it myself because I never ask for help if I think I can do something myself," replied Chester. He drove into the farmyard and stopped the car under a tree.

Tamra moved closer, and after he turned off the headlights, his arm went around her neck. The next moment, as if by magic, they were kissing. She had a different perfume on.

"Hold me tighter," Tamra whispered.

"Don't rush me," he replied.

No more was said for some minutes, and then she left the car for her room.

"See you later. Goodnight, Chester!" Tamra wore an orange sweater and brown slacks.

"Goodnight, sweetheart!" he replied. It was the first time he had called her that. A full moon emerged from some clouds, and he watched her walk up the sidewalk.

The couple sat together in church on Sunday, and then Monday arrived. The crops were all in for the year, and the only field work left before winter was disking the corn stalks and plowing the cornfield.

Chester had just gotten off the school bus and changed clothes. He mounted the tractor near the gas barrel.

The disk was hooked up behind. Chester had a single shot, twenty gauge, Stevens model 1913 shotgun along because it was pheasant hunting season. He made a few rounds on the tractor, and then he espied a ring-necked pheasant among the corn stalk rows. He took a steady aim and fired once and the bird flopped over like a sack of potatoes.

When he returned to the farmyard, Ole cleaned the bird for the next meal.

It had rained on Tuesday, and since the ground was too wet for fieldwork, Louie and Chester took their weapons to go hunting. They looked along the ground when they hunted instead of up in the trees. Those big red, corn-fed fox squirrels were two times as big as their little gray cousins seen in cities. Even the country gray squirrels were a lot bigger than their city-bred cousins.

The brothers crossed a barbed wire fence in reaching the big woods; they were wearing jackets and caps. They looked forward to hunting each year.

"Have you got some extra shells?" asked Louie.

"Yep, I can give you a few," said Chester. "Let's separate. You take the right, and I can go straight ahead."

"Okay, let's meet back here by this pond in an hour," replied Louie.

They then took different paths. Each had telescopes on his .22 rifle. Chester espied a squirrel running along a dead log, and then it rushed up a tree half covered with gold and scarlet leaves. He dropped the red one with one blast. By the end of the day, Chester had fired six shots and had gotten five.

He also had seen a red fox, a deer, chipmunks, and a brown woodchuck near a sinkhole. He bagged the latter animal for the fifteen-cent bounty. That would buy in return, a bottle of soda pop and a candy bar.

Louie got four squirrels and had seen a deer on the run.

Ole dressed out the meat, and it went into the freezer. The hunters had seen many squirrels gathering nuts for the winter ahead.

During the following days, the brothers and Ole completed the plowing and disking in the fields. Louie and Chester helped when school was out.

The weather was mild on a late autumn day when there was a football game. Chester finished chores early and drove to the high school. Under the lights, the female cheerleaders in green, white, and gold were jumping up and down like western jackrabbits; it was as if they had ants in their pants.

Tamra Hunt was among them, and since it was a small rustic farming community, all the players and cheerleaders were white people, namely, Norwegians, Irish, Scotch, and German with the former being dominant in numbers.

Summer Mirage

Then the football players came onto the field; they included Rusty Wampuch, a guard. They were playing a rival, the Peterson Tigers. The latter got the kickoff and marched to the fifteen-yard line, and Rusty made the tackle. The Tigers then kicked a field goal. The Rushford Trojan cheerleaders cheered and shouted, "Cage the Tigers!"

Then the Trojans scored on a pass play that covered half the gridiron, and Rusty made a key block. The rest of the game was a defensive struggle. The Trojans won by the score of seven to three. Later, there was a dance at the gym.

While Tamra, still in her uniform, was dancing with Chester, they espied Rusty swinging his new girlfriend, Molly Olson, and dancing superbly. She was a brunette and two grades below him. Soon, the four students got into Rusty's car, a green 1953 De Soto. They stopped at a root beer stand.

"That was a good game you played, Rusty," said Chester.

"I was lucky a couple of times," he replied.

"What do you mean?" asked Molly.

"I did not hit the ball carrier hard, but he fell down."

"Maybe you don't know your own strength," added Chester.

"Let's all of us attend a drive-in movie tomorrow night," suggested Molly.

"A good idea! How about it?" asked Tamra.

"Great, I will drive!" responded Chester.

As they drove home, a few songs came on the radio: "The Wayward Wind" by Gogi Grant, "Cross Over the Bridge" by Patty Page, and "Pittsburg, Pennsylvania" by Guy Mitchell.

Rusty left Chester and Tamra off at the school and then took Molly home. Another school week had ended.

A brisk wind blew up during the night with some rain.

It was Saturday, and Chester spent the day looking at TV. After doing a take home class assignment, he picked up his girl Tamra and Rusty and Molly. The girls wore sweaters and slacks, while the boys were in Levis and warm flannel shirts.

Playing at the outdoor theater was Zane Grey's, Robber's Roost, a colorful western starring the rugged cast of Peter Graves, Jim Davis, and Sylvia Findley. They arrived just before the cartoon began, and next the previews came on screen. When the feature film was about to begin, Rusty and Chester rushed to the snack bar for pop and popcorn. Then they witnessed the two outlaw gangs fight for control of ranch land.

As Tamra lay snugly against Chester, he glanced at the back seat to see Rusty and Molly in a similar position. It seemed as though every time the action died down on the silver screen, the action livened up in the car. The scene was cozy.

After a few warm kisses, Chester rose up and looked around.

"What is the matter?" asked Tamra.

"I am missing too much of the movie, and I paid money to see it!"

"Chester is right," said Molly. "It is a good movie!"

She and Rusty also sat up, and they all saw the end of the movie.

A double feature was playing there in the river valley of the Mississippi, in the city of Winona, where fog would rise from the lake and river on cold autumn mornings.

The second movie was a Jerry Lewis and Dean Martin comedy in a western setting called "Partners".

The group drove to their homes after the film ended, and it was late when Chester entered his long gravel driveway. He shook hands with Adolf, the dog. That animal had a couple of female friends in the rural neighborhood and was gone sometimes. Maybe Adolf had more cozy secrets than his masters had.

The sky was cloudy, and Chester could see some stars and the Big Dipper between the sailing clouds high over the house. It was chilly outside. A yellow cat screeched near the barn, and Adolf lifted his ears to listen. A cow had probably stepped on a cat's tail or a foot.

Chester climbed the stairs for his bedroom.

A strong, cold wind rose during the night, and in the early morning as Chester looked out the window, he saw that the ground was white with snow. No more fieldwork until April!

It was Sunday, and he was going hunting in the forest. He headed off for the woods, carrying his old Stevens gun. The snow was not yet deep. He espied woodpeckers, blue jays, blackbirds, and chipmunks. Adolf was not much of a dog hunter for game, so Chester trekked among the trees alone. The place looked like a picture postcard.

Then he saw a cottontail rabbit bounce along, and when it stopped, he blasted away. The distance was short, so it blew off half the rabbit's head. Chester picked it up and looked for more game. He soon came upon a sinkhole; he crept up slowly and had the gun ready. A big red fox ran off at the sight of the intruder, and Chester fired his single shot antique shotgun, leveling the fox to the white ground.

It was getting cold as he sat down on a log to sip some coffee from a jug. Chester heard a noise nearby and saw three squirrels playing on the ground. He moved closer and picked off one from a tree trunk. He shot the second one as it climbed an oak tree. The next one disappeared, but he circled the trees slowly. Most of the leaves were shed and lay under the snow.

Then the hunter espied a fluffy tail high up in the tree. He backtracked ten yards and could see most of the big red squirrel. Chester placed his gun against a tree to steady it. As he squeezed the trigger, the shotgun belched lead pellets, fire, and smoke. The animal went flying like an airplane as the lead hit it. He went over to pick it up and headed home, carrying the squirrels, a fox, and a rabbit.

A big, snowy, white owl stared at Chester as he walked by an animal path in the woods. He soon reached a clearing and crossed over the barbed wire fence. A snowplow was traveling on the road pushing the snow into a ditch. Ole did the cleaning of the game, while Chester got a bounty for the fox.

He had almost forgotten that it was his birthday. When he went in for supper, Lucy had an angel food cake with candles on top.

"Did you see anything in the woods?" she asked.

"I had a good day of hunting," he replied.

Chester's eyes glittered as he saw the gifts. He opened a box to see an ancient Roman chess set, and in another box were a fishing rod and reel. He was real happy on that winter day.

"I will be using this in the spring when the trout season opens!"

"You could go ice fishing on the river or lake," said Ole.

"I am afraid the ice would break. Well, I will have to show my friends my presents," replied his son.

That night, while Ole and Chester were in the barn milking the cows and throwing down hay, a blizzard developed. It started to blow from the west, and visibility was almost zero. The snow was coming down. While Chester was up in the hayloft, he grabbed a few sparrows in the semi-darkness and finished them off by dashing them against the barn roof. He tossed them down a hay chute, and the cats had a feast.

As he was climbing down the chute, the barn door opened along with a gust of wind and snow flurries, admitting Rusty, Sam, and Bruce. Chester felt a chill.

"Happy birthday, Chester!" they all said in unison.

"Are you all out on a bad night like this?" he asked.

"Sam and I love snow storms; the worse the weather is, the better we like it!" said Rusty.

"Why is that?" asked Chester.

"It toughens a person and builds character!"

"That is interesting," replied the host.

Louie entered and helped with chores.

"How about a card game and some drinking tonight?" asked Bruce.

They all wore mackinaw coats and winter caps.

"I am game; Ole left the barn just before you guys came, and he and Lucy are going away for supper. We got the house all to ourselves tonight," explained Chester.

Since all were farmers and friends, they helped finish the chores. Rusty and Sam helped spread out the hay in front of the dairy cows, while Bruce Thompson rinsed out the utensils in the milk house. Soon, they were walking towards the house as the big storm continued its force.

Rusty picked up a package from his 1953 green De Soto car. They were present to help Chester have a good time on his birthday.

"What have you got there?" asked Chester.

"Good-tasting booze!" he said.

They all entered the house.

Summer Mirage

Rusty placed two six packs of Bub's beer on the table, and Bruce pulled out a bottle of Scotch whiskey from his coat. Then all sat around a card table as the host shuffled the cards. The game was Rook, and Chester and Rusty stood against Sam and Bruce.

They were drinking beer as the latter got the kitty on the first round. Rusty had a good hand in yellow and had the high cards of thirteen and fourteen. Chester bid forty in red later on. The teenagers finished the beer by the third game, and then they started on the whiskey and Seven-Up to make high balls. Each side won a couple of games since no players dominated.

"Remember when we were in elementary school, and we played cowboys and Indians in the woods?" asked Chester.

"Yeah, and you could yell both the Sioux and Comanche war cries," said Sam. "Let us hear you do it again, just for old times sake!"

"All right," replied Chester. "Hoka-haa! Kannee-Wah, Fury!"

The friends all clapped their hands.

"What was the 'Fury' for?" asked Rusty.

"That's the name of my horse."

As their drinking kept on, so did the taking chances in bidding and playing.

"Hey, I am feeling great!" said Sam.

"I believe you are drunk," said his brother.

"Who me? Hell, no!" Then Bruce leaned his head across the table and emitted a loud belch.

"Watch it, you pig," said Rusty in jest.

The latter could take the booze better than anyone without showing any effects.

"Where did Louie go tonight?" asked Bruce.

"He went with my folks for supper at the Hot Fish Shop in Winona," said the host.

"I can play cards better when I am drunk," stated Rusty.

"I can bowl better after I have had a few beers," said Sam.

A musical featuring Guy Lombardo and his Royal Canadians was on television. Singing was Dinah Shore, a blonde who had become a big star during World War Two. She complemented the smooth music of the orchestra.

The boys played cards until they were too drunk to remember whose turn it was to throw down a card. Rusty and Bruce hugged each other as they started for a couch.

They never made it because they fell on the floor and then laughed at themselves. Sam was sitting with his head on a card table, quite drunk. Chester was leaning back in his chair and saw Dinah singing "The Yellow Rose of Texas."

"I guess you boys will have to stay here tonight because you would not get far in this snowstorm," said Chester.

They were snowbound on Chester's birthday in December. Meanwhile, Dinah was singing "Silent Night" and then "Jingle Bells." It was one in the morning when Rusty and Bruce tried climbing the stairs. They were as drunk as a couple of rabid skunks, and it was a great task to reach the second floor.

The blizzard subsided after the boys turned off the lights and pulled up the blankets. Sam slept on the davenport, while Chester occupied the downstairs bedroom.

Ole, Lucy, and Louie spent the night at Alice and Lester's farm where they had a good time playing "500" at cards.

As the wind died down, a timber wolf from the north woods crept around the side of the house looking for food. Adolf slept in the barn during the winter, or else there would have been a big fight with the wolf for the fish and chicken bones left over from supper.

Chapter Thirteen

The next morning, the boys got up later than usual, and all had headaches. They experienced their first hangovers. The door was opened to show a huge snowdrift and wolf tracks.

The sky was sunny with a cold breeze, and the air was invigorating. Too many deep breaths of it would cause a cold and sore throat because the temperature was twenty degrees below zero Fahrenheit.

The foursome put on their coats, caps, boots, and mittens to go outside. They stepped into the deep snow and headed for the barn.

"I should not have drank so much beer and whiskey last night," said Sam. He was not feeling so well.

Everyone looked pale. The teenagers made short work of the chores. The barn was fairly warm from the animal heat.

"We cannot get home until the snowplow comes," said Rusty.

"That goes for my folks too," added Chester.

After the work was done, they noted that a cow had given birth to a calf prematurely. Since it would die anyway, Bruce dragged it outside and left it to freeze to death. The steam was coming off the wet hide of the calf as it lay bellowing.

Then the friends entered the big, white house for breakfast.

"The best thing to sober up on is milk," said Rusty, who always had good ideas under his red head of hair.

"That is just what I need!" said Sammy.

Chester got a pitcher from the refrigerator and poured four glasses of milk.

Bruce prepared the bacon and eggs in a fry pan, while the host made pancakes and got out a box of Wheaties with a baseball player on the cover. Just because there were no ladies in the house to do the cooking, they were not going hungry.

On the wall hung a gold-colored calendar with historic dates on it, including birthdays of presidents, generals, and big events. The big red letters on top read: "Rushford State Bank."

"That food sure smells good! I don't know if I can eat a full meal though, but being outside for an hour builds up an eager appetite," said Rusty.

He and Sam did the dishes after the meal, while Bruce and Chester put on some musical records on the Decca phonograph. They all heard Gene Autry singing "Sioux City Sue" and "Up on the Housetop" and Roy Rogers singing "Happy Trails to You."

"Roy, Gene, John Wayne, and Randolf Scott are the best actors in the movies," said Bruce.

"And Marilyn Monroe, Mary Murphy, Debra Paget, and Pier Angeli are the best actresses," added Chester.

Suddenly, they heard a noise outside as they espied a snow plow on the road. It had tough going as it hit a large drift, but the driver backed up and surged ahead in full speed. Then he made it through the snowdrift.

"I guess we can get through to go home now," said Bruce. "I would like to ride your horse once before I leave."

"It will be a cold ride, and don't forget that George Washington went horseback riding in December and got a bad cold and died in 1799," stated Chester.

"I will not be on Fury long," replied his pal.

The foursome returned to the barn to saddle up Chester's palomino.

"I traded a paint horse for this one," said Chester. "I called that other horse "Beauty," he added.

Fury was munching on hay in his stall. Soon, Chester led his golden horse outside where Bruce climbed on his back.

"Steady boy!" said the rider. He neck reined the sturdy horse down the driveway and out onto the gravel road. The trio looked at the horse and rider run in a gallop. The owner was a little worried because there were still snow and ice on the road, but Bruce and Fury returned safely.

"How do you like him?" asked Chester.

"I don't know since I did not taste him yet," replied Bruce in good humor. "I think your horse is great, next to mine," he added.

"Do you want to ride Fury?" Chester asked Sam.

"Heck no, I don't want to freeze my hinder off, but maybe when the weather warms up."

They all went to the house where the youths got their belongings and then took their leave.

"See you at school on Monday if it does not drift too much!" Rusty called out while getting into his car.

"Happy trails to you!" replied Chester while peering out from the front door.

Sam came running back to the house, saying, "I forgot my mittens!"

"Happy hunting!" he added after grabbing his mittens.

Chester went to the barn after his friends had gone.

Then his folks and Louie returned and parked in the red garage. Lucy wore a brown-colored fur coat.

"I thought you had gone on your second honeymoon last night," said Chester.

"It almost seemed like we did," said Lucy.

"Did you get the work done all right?" queried Ole.

"Oh yeah, and I had a lot of help because Rusty, Sam, and Bruce came to help me celebrate my birthday, and they stayed overnight!"

Ole took off his gray-colored mackinaw coat.

"We were worried that you would not have any help with the chores," his mother said.

"That's what good country neighbors are for! All's well that ends well," added Chester.

That weekend, Chester did his homework with the English and history books.

Soon, it was the day before Christmas. The Borseth family drove to the big city of Rochester for some last-minute Christmas shopping. Chester bought a box of candy for Lucy, and he thought he would play a joke on Ole by getting him a box of Ex-Lax laxative besides the Copenhagen snuff for gifts.

The brothers attended a double feature movie at the old Lawler Theater, the first being "Cattle Queen of Montana" with Ronald Reagan and Barbara Stanwyck. It was a good rip-roaring western movie. Then they saw Pier Angeli and Paul Newman in "Somebody Up There Likes Me" in which Paul played a boxer.

"Pier has a good foreign accent," said Chester.

Before they went home, Louie and Lucy went to buy groceries, while Ole and Chester entered a tavern.

"Do you want a Tom and Jerry drink?" asked Ole. "It is a Christmas drink made with brandy, egg whites, and spices."

"I am still a teenager; will the bartender allow it?" asked Chester, as he removed his gray mackinaw coat.

"He don't give a damn because he wants to sell all the liquor he can," explained Ole.

The drink was hot, strong, and delicious.

"How much did the movies cost?" asked Ole while drinking his Tom and Jerry.

"It cost me thirty-five cents, plus a dime for a candy bar."

Louie helped his mother carry the groceries to the Chevy car, and they left for home. After doing chores, all changed clothes again in preparation for church.

Chester put on his tan-colored suit, a white shirt, and a blue necktie. The family drove a few miles across the fields of white-covered earth and made it in time for the Christmas Eve service. There were two large balsam fir trees up front that were decorated with lights, silver tinsel, and bells of blue, green, red, and gold. There were presents under one tree.

The children spoke, then sang Christmas carols, and gave verse readings. That was the annual tradition of the church. On the way

Summer Mirage

home later, Chester saw a man carrying a sack on his back from a garage to a house.

It looked like Santa Claus out there in farm country. The Borseths arrived home and put on the lights as Lucy brought out candy, nuts, and drinks. Everyone started opening gifts. Chester received a box of candy and clothes. Ole opened his box of Ex-Lax, and they all had a laugh. The well-decorated conifer was a Norway pine tree.

"That long package by the wall is yours," said Lucy.

Chester took it and removed the colorful wrapping. A blue barrel emerged, then a brown stock. It was a new 30-30 model Winchester rifle, the gun some men said had won the West.

"Now I can go deer hunting up north," he gladly announced.

"You can hunt more than deer with it too," added Louie. He got a new motorbike that Santa had brought him.

The family then ate and drank a few goodies and watched television on a dark brown Philco set. The Mormon Tabernacle choir was singing carols on the idiot box. To see a movie in color, one had to drive to a movie show theater.

Ole received a grain shovel, and Lucy got a pretty dress.

Santa Claus was generous that year as each person got four gifts. The boys set their presents by a window and went to bed.

Chester rose early on Christmas morning to see the sky rosy and gold. The temperature had risen, and there was a heat wave of twenty degrees above zero Fahrenheit. Chester and Adolf raced for the barn, and the dog won, as usual. The dog did sleep in the barn at night if he wanted to, where it was warm and cozy from the body heat of the cattle and horses, but sometimes he lay outside on the porch.

Chester began to milk the cows and poured milk into a pan for the hungry cats.

After the milk truck had come and gone, and the bulk tank was scrubbed clean, the men returned to the house. It was late in the morning, and Lucy had duck in the oven.

A car entered the driveway, tooting a horn. It was Les, Alice, and Bernie in an Oldsmobile, a brown 1953 Model; they were coming for

Christmas dinner. Lucy opened the door, and after the usual greetings, everyone was seated in the dining room of the large Victorian home.

They had just come from church, and Les was in a brown suit, Bernie in a light blue suit, and Alice in an orange outfit. The house was decorated for the holidays.

"I heard you had a party here one night," said Les.

"I guess you can call it that," replied Chester.

"Was it a stag party?" queried Bernie.

"Yeah, there were no girls."

"What did you get for Christmas, Bernie?" asked Louie.

"Clothes and snow tires."

Alice joined Lucy in the kitchen. "I went to a classmate's wedding last Saturday," said Alice.

"Which one?" asked Lucy.

"It was Brenda and a home insulation contractor who won her heart," said her daughter. "It was a small wedding with the bride and groom, one best man and the bridesmaid," added Alice, the older sister of Chester and Louie.

The women were preparing the big feast.

"Well, how is everything going with the chickens and cattle, Ole?" asked Lester.

"We just culled out a hundred hens and sold them, and we are milking cows, and they fill the bulk tank every two days," replied the farm owner. "We have fifty milk cows."

"I am going to sell a load of hogs next week," said Les.

"Can you all stand a mixed drink before dinner?" asked Ole.

"Oh, hell, yes, I'm as thirsty as a sweaty nigger hoeing a cotton field in Alabama," spoke up Bernie Baker.

"I'm ready for a drink," said Les.

"Let's haul in the drinks," said Louie.

Father and son went to the kitchen and grabbed ice from the refrigerator and Blackjack mix from the pantry and Sunnybrook whiskey from a cupboard. After mixing the drinks, Louie handed Bernie a glass and his big, red, bloodshot eyes held on the drink.

"Thanks, Louie," he said.

"You bet!"

Soon, Alice and Lucy, the two farm wives, were bringing in food and putting it on the long table. The duck took up a large portion of the space, and it was a banquet equal to Easter or Thanksgiving day.

"It is ready; everyone sit up to the table now," said Lucy while smiling.

The clan all took chairs and dug in with each person helping himself; they sat for about an hour.

They then filed into the next room, and Chester turned on the television set. A college football game was on the boob tube without color.

"I could never understand that game," said Ole.

"Look at the way them idiots pile up on each other; isn't it stupid?" added Les.

The men looked at the game for a while; then Ole asked, "How about a beer?"

Everyone replied, "Yeah!"

Ole returned from the kitchen with four bottles of Bub's beer brewed next to Sugarloaf Bluff in the city of Winona.

After a time of drinking and munching on candy and being couch potatoes for an afternoon in front of the TV set, the men rose up to stroll out to a poll shed to look at some steers. A few well-fed Hereford cattle with white heads and brown hides were in a pen, and Bernie opened the gate and entered for a closer look.

"Hey, this one looks pretty good!" he said as he put a hand on its rump. The husky steer lurched up and gave Bernie a swift kick on his leg.

"Oww, God damn bastard steer!" he uttered in pain.

The men laughed at the humor, and that was the funniest event they saw on Christmas Day. The group entered the barn and Bernie tried to clean the manure from his suit pants. They looked at a huge black and white Holstein bull in a pen.

"I would not want to tangle with him," said Les.

"I am going to sell him soon because he is getting too big and surly to handle," stated Ole.

Bernie looked at a pocket watch and said, "It's pudner five."

"Let's hit the road," responded Les.

They walked to the house, and the Greys got out their box of gifts and placed them under the pine Christmas tree.

"We almost forget the main thing we came for -- the gifts," said Alice.

They all got more presents, and the paper piled up on the rug. The scene was merry, and everyone gloated over the booty. Lucy brought out bottles of soda pop for all.

It was dusk when they grabbed their coats and gifts and left for home. The afterglow of sunset was still over the forest.

Ole and his sons still had chores to do on holidays. Then after a couple of hours in the barn and poultry house, Chester changed back into his Sunday clothes. He backed his Chevy out of the garage and headed for the home of Tamra Hunt.

Her mother, June, let him in and he sat a few minutes to wait for his date. The gorgeous auburn-haired lady came down the stairs in a red sweater and brown slacks. Chester then compared her to one other sweater girl, Marilyn Monroe.

"Are you dressed up warm enough?" he asked.

"I got a good winter fur coat," she said. "A brown one."

While on the road, Chester's favorite girl said, "Why not do something different tonight? Saint Teresa College in Winona is putting on a stage play, Uncle Tom's Cabin."

"Okay, we will go to see it," he replied.

They arrived just as the curtain opened and sat in row five. At intermission, they went to the lobby for glasses of punch.

The play adapted from Harriet Stowe's novel helped bring on the American Civil War. They left for home as the curtain closed. While walking up her sidewalk, they saw the lights glowing on the white pine Christmas tree.

"Come in for a while and see what I got for Christmas," said Tamra.

Under the tree, Chester saw clothes, candy, perfume, a pen set, and a diary.

"How do you like the new suit I got from Santa?" Tamra asked.

Summer Mirage

"The style is novel, and the purple color looks good on you," answered Chester.

"Help yourself to some nuts, candy, and a bottle of Seven-Up," suggested Tamra.

The table was loaded with goodies.

The lady turned on the TV, and a movie, "Broken Arrow", was on; it was a superb western starring Debra Paget and James Stewart. The couple relaxed on the davenport to view the Arizona setting.

"We had a lot of company here today as many of my goofy relatives came for the big feast, and they were hungry as a pack of dogs," she said.

"We had company too, my sister Alice and Lester. You should of seen that steer kick Bernie in his leg when he put a hand on its rump. I had a good laugh," said Chester.

They sat in silence for a while and looked at the show on television. It had a sad ending as the heroine died, and Stewart rode off alone into the sunset. Then Chester got his coat and paused with Tamra at a door under the green mistletoe.

Their arms were around each other, and cheeks were touching. Then their lips met, and they stood for a while.

"It was a good Christmas," said Chester.

"The best I ever had," replied his sweetheart. The lights highlighted her hair.

It might have been an eternity, but they released their holds, and Chester walked out into the glistening snow. It had gotten colder, and the air was invigorating.

The past summer almost seems like a dream or a mirage, said Chester to himself.

Chapter Fourteen

A couple of weeks later, it was a bright, sunny day in January, and Bernie was driving towards Chicago.

"By gosh, it was good of Les to give me a one-week paid vacation," said Bernie out loud.

He stopped at Madison for lunch and walked into a nice restaurant and espied on a shelf some model tractors and trucks of many makes. It was similar to a museum.

"Alice was always talking about Chicago, and I have never been there," said Bernie.

After he had lunch, the trip continued, and soon he was in the great city of the Midwest and driving on Michigan Avenue near the lake and past the Art Institute. He parked at the Cass Hotel, famous as the best little hotel in the city. Bernie encountered a desk clerk who was watching the Chet Huntley and David Brinkley news report.

"Do you have a room for me?" he inquired.

"Number five on this floor and here is the key," the aged man replied.

Bernie carried his suitcase in and made himself comfortable. After a short rest, he found the street that led to a saloon and upon entering, sat down at the bar. In a corner were musicians playing a guitar, a cello, and a piano.

Summer Mirage

"Give me a cold bottle of Schlitz beer," said Bernie. He noticed a lady with her back to him, and Bernie thought he had seen that head of dark hair before.

She turned around, and it was Sally Benson. She wore a green dress.

"Holy shits, when did you get here?" he asked.

"So it's Bernie, of all people, you old villain. I arrived here two days ago on my vacation. Sit down to join me," said Sally. "What the hell are you doing in Chicago, Bernie?"

"Les gave me a week off from work. Two more drinks," he ordered.

"Coming right up," replied the cute redhead bartender in a red dress. She returned with two bottles of Schlitz beer.

"Did you have a good Christmas day?" asked Bernie.

"It was okay, but it could have been better. It's the same old story every year, the same songs and church services. I get a few gifts that I don't need, eat a little extra and that is about it," explained Sally. She grabbed a few peanuts from a bowl.

"It don't mean much to me either. You should have seen all the food at the Ole and Lucy Borseth farm; it was a real feast on Christmas day," commented Bernie.

They listened to the live music for a spell.

"How about joining me in my hotel room?" Bernie suggested.

"All right," replied Sally with a smile.

"It is so windy," she said later while walking down the sidewalk.

Bernie held on to his hat so it would not blow off his head. He bought a newspaper as they saw a gift shop in the hotel lobby.

Back in his room, Bernie laughed while reading the comic pages.

Constable's "The Haywain" painting was hanging on the wall.

"I am going to the bathroom to comb my hair," said Sally.

Ten minutes later, she returned and faced Bernie who was reading.

"How do you like me now?" she asked.

He put down the paper to look at her. The brunette was standing with a dearth of clothes, not even a stocking on. Bernie was startled at first, and then he smiled. "That's more like it," he replied.

Sally flipped a light and sat on the bed. He could still make out her form and joined Sally at the bedside. Little was said during the next hour as nature took its course. The closed windows shut out the noise from the street.

Around midnight, both people lay back on the bed relaxed and happy. He rose about nine in the morning and nudged his friend. She also rose and entered the shower. They then put on nice clothes and went to breakfast.

"It is a lovely day to go for a ride," said the lady.

"Yeah, life is short, so let's go and see the sights."

That day the two friends visited the Art Institute, the Lincoln Park Zoo, and the Shedd Aquarium.

As the vacationers were leaving the last place, Sally said, "This has been an interesting day. I did not think there were that many fish in the whole world."

Bernie and Sally lived together for the next few days and nights driving all over the windy city of Chicago. They went to a baseball game at Wrigley Field and saw the Cubs play the Milwaukee Braves, featuring Henry Aaron, Eddie Matthews, and the high leg-raising pitcher, Warren Spahn. Ernie Banks of the Cubs, Matthews, and "Hammering Hank" hit home runs.

It was the weekend, and the duo was back at the Cass Hotel.

"May I ride back to Minnesota with you?" asked Sally.

"Why sure you can," said Bernie while packing his suitcase. He left the key at a desk in the lobby on the way out. They then stopped for food at a truck stop in the suburb of St. Charles and parked his green 1951 Hudson car.

"This looks like a good place to eat." He ordered a good working man's breakfast of ham and eggs.

"Just give me toast, jelly, and coffee," Sally told the fat waitress. "What are you looking at?" she asked.

"Look out the window and see that tall man in a tan western suit and a white cowboy hat stepping out of his Cadillac car with a Texas license plate," said Bernie. "I wonder what he does for a living?"

"He is either a rancher or an oil man, like Rock Hudson or James Dean in the movie, Giant," replied Sally.

Summer Mirage

The couple took a different route home, driving past the town of Clinton, Iowa, and then they traveled a road north to Dubuque. After a while, Bernie was getting sleepy, and his foot became heavy.

They crossed the Minnesota state line and were cruising towards Caledonia, the town with a Roman name. Bernie did not see the sharp curve up ahead, and his car went through a fence and rolled over in a ditch. It was dented up badly.

A while later, he came to his senses and was bloody and in pain. His eyes almost popped out of his sockets, like the black man in the freak show at the State Fair, when he saw Sally, crushed under his green car. She was as dead as an old, dusty mummy in a pyramid.

Bernie became panic stricken in that horrible accident. He tried to pull his lady out from under his car.

"Holy fart suckers, what have I done?" he asked.

A highway patrolman was on the scene soon to investigate. He radioed for an ambulance. Soon, Bernie heard the siren and saw the flashing red lights. He felt himself being given first aid and carried in a stretcher. At night he lay in a bed at a hospital.

"How bad am I, Doc?" he asked a man in a white jacket.

"I cannot find any broken bones on you. The nurse will be on you like an eagle eye tonight, and you will be able to go home soon," said the doctor.

"She can be on me any way she wants to," returned Bernie.

"Ha, ha, at least you got a sense of humor," replied the doctor.

A pretty nurse gave him a cup of water, saying, "Drink this."

"I don't give a brown bull turd about myself; it's Sally."

"Yeah, I understand how you feel, and it was too bad about your lovely companion, but I don't think she suffered long," said the wise doctor.

Bernie lay there in gloom all night. Strange thoughts went past his mind. A speeding car, the fence, glaring red lights, and the hotel room back in the Queen city of the Midwest, Chicago.

By morning, he was out of the hospital wearing bandages, and he caught a bus for Rushford. Upon reaching the hamlet nestled between

Rush Creek, the Root River, and wooded bluffs, he called Les on a telephone from the old corner hotel.

"I was in an accident; can you come and pick me up?" Bernie asked.

"Okay, I will be in town in an hour, after I slop the hogs," replied Lester.

Bernie waited for his boss while having a cup of coffee and a donut at the Niggle Cafe. Les soon arrived.

"Hey, you look like you had a bad accident."

"My car is wrecked, and my friend, Sally, got killed," said Bernie.

"The hell you say. I don't think I ever met her," Les commented.

After they hopped in Les' car, Les said to the man near his own age, "You can rest up for a couple of days."

Bernie went to bed upon arriving at the Lester Grey farm, and the boss fed livestock and did the daily chores. Alice put a chocolate cake in the oven and turned on the Philco TV set to watch "Matinee Theater."

I will help Les milk the cows tonight since Bernie is laid up, she said to herself.

Two days later, the hired man felt better physically, but not mentally. Bernie worked in the barn for a few days, throwing down silage and hay, milking and cleaning the barn, feeding the pigs, and then shoveling snow from the driveway. He was getting thirsty.

One night, he went upstairs and put on a bright sport shirt and light colored slacks. He took leave while Alice was washing the dishes.

"Are you going out tonight?" she asked while wiping a plate.

"Yeah, I want to play some pool," replied Bernie.

He got into the used car he had just bought since he had smashed up two previous cars. Bernie now had a brown 1952 Nash. He took a road for Winona.

He parked next to the "Hurryback" pool hall and played a game. Later, he entered a bar at the Williams Hotel.

"Give me a Hamm's beer," he ordered.

A bartender brought a bottle to him. "How about a dollar button for the Winter Carnival?"

Summer Mirage

"Okay, I will buy one," said Bernie.

There was a goofy guy at the bar who was laughing loud and talking a lot. He took a broom and went behind the bar to chase the fat bartender, but was not serious, only jesting. He then settled down.

The bartender switched the RCA model TV to, "Your Hit Parade," with blonde Dorothy Collins and Gisele McKensie, a brunette. Dorothy sang Eddie Fisher's song, "You Gotta Have Heart." Then Gisele sang "The Naughty Lady of Shady Lane."

After some time, Bernie was drunk with his head lowered on the bar. Not able to drive, he staggered to a hotel room. It was the start of one of his drunken periods. He lay on the bed and pulled up a blanket and stayed there until late the next morning.

Feeling better by noon, he went to a nearby restaurant called "Ruth's Place" and had a cup of hot tea and a Danish roll. He brought back a Straight Arrow comic book to his hotel room. He had listened to the radio program of the same name.

Outside, a snowstorm had developed, and big snowflakes were being driven by a brisk wind, and snowdrifts were piling up. Bernie rose from his bed just as the sun set, like Count Dracula, and he walked to a tavern on Mankato Avenue; it was on the east side of Winona in the Pollock section.

That place had its goofy barflies at the bar also.

Bernie ordered brandy with Coca-Cola.

"I think you need glasses since your eyes are so red. Maybe you are straining them," the pretty bartender in a yellow dress told him.

"I will strain you," he replied.

She gave him a strange look and left.

He sat for a long spell until the bartender told him to leave, saying that he had had enough to drink. Bernie then staggered out into the falling snow; everything was white on the ground.

A teenage boy and girl sat in a car watching Bernie, the drunk. He was facing them as he leaned onto a building for balance; he then jerked out his cock and urinated on the ground. The couple in the car laughed. Bernie did not notice them as he walked another half block before lying down on the sidewalk.

A policeman came and asked him, "What is the matter here?"

"Go and hit the road, or I will put my ass in your face and blow a cannon fart, making you a casualty!" said Bernie.

The cop and bystanders all laughed like African hyenas at his uncommon remark. The young couple that were in the car came over to tell what they had seen. The blue uniformed cop then took Bernie by the arm and led him to the police station.

Later, the captain rang the telephone of Les Grey, saying, "We got your hired man here in the jailhouse," he informed Les.

"I am not going to bail him out this time. If he has not learned his lesson, it's his hard luck," replied Les.

"All right, so long Mr. Grey," said the cop.

Bernie slept again in jail, lying down on the metal floor and using his shoes for a pillow. He saw a dozen men in one long cell with a toilet at one end. Two cops brought in a husky young man.

After they left, he was shaking and rattling the door. The cops returned and manhandled him into a separate cell. The youth had tattoos on his arms. Bernie received bread and water, and then lay back on his shirt and shoes.

Then all through the night, he heard the men blowing book-slamming farts and booming-cannon farts. It seemed like a contest to see who could fart the loudest. Everyone wanted to be the world champion and win a trophy. An open window provided some ventilation for better air.

At breakfast, Bernie was given oatmeal with no milk or sugar. He asked for milk, but never got it.

"Those dumb shit cops never saw the pint of Old Crow whiskey that I got in my pocket," Bernie said to an inmate.

Later, he got so careless that a cop discovered the jug.

The guard on duty opened the cell door and took the bottle.

He drank a swig from Bernie's jug saying, "This bourbon is nice and smooth!"

"Give me a swig of that," another cop said.

The two cops got drunk and staggered around the jailhouse.

The next day, Bernie was led to a car by two law officers.

"Where are we going?" he asked them.

"We are taking you to a happy place," said the tall cop.

The car entered Highway 14 and headed west. They passed by Hilltop, Stockton, the Archess Park, and then the mostly German hamlet of Lewiston, and the car never stopped until they reached Rochester. They approached some brick buildings, and Bernie espied a woman petting a tree.

"What the hell is this place?" he asked.

"The State Insane Asylum," the driver replied.

"You are not taking me to the God damn nut house!" objected Bernie, getting flushed in the face.

"I have the official papers here that authorize us to take you here, so don't try anything stupid," warned the cop.

"Son-of-a-bitch...God damn it!" uttered Bernie, becoming perplexed.

After parking, they took him into the building and met the chief person in psychiatry.

"I am crazy," said the tall cop.

The doctor nodded and came closer to the trio. "I understand," said the medical man.

Two white-robed men came and led the hired man away.

Later, the short deputy asked the other one who had talked to the doctor, "Why did you say that you are crazy?"

"A sick person would never admit that he is crazy, so that is why the psychiatrist knew what I meant when I told him I am crazy."

From a window, Bernie watched the law officers leave. The gold and purple sunset with a silver lining seemed like a mirage because it kept changing by the minute. Then dusk settled in the western sky.

Chapter Fifteen

Some months had gone by, and it was deer hunting season in November. A blue 1952 Chevrolet halted at a gas station in Rochester, Minnesota. Chester Borseth, Bruce Thompson, Rusty, and Sam Wampuch stepped out of the car to stretch. They were across from the Miracle Mile Shopping Center.

"I better fill it up because we got a long ways to go before we reach Warroad," said Chester, the driver.

"How close it that to Canada?" asked Sammy.

"It is on the border and Lake of the Woods," replied Rusty. "Here is three dollars from each of us to help pay on the gas."

Chester put the money in his pocket.

"Do you think we have enough ammunition along?" queried the oldest of the teens, Bruce.

"If we don't, we can buy more up north," responded the boy with the great ideas, Rusty.

"Maybe we won't see many deer anyway," added Sam, the youngest of the group. He was sometimes a clever pessimist.

After the grease monkey put gas in the car and took a look under the hood, the youths were on the road again. They had a canvass tent and sleeping bags in the trunk.

"I can't wait to put my Winchester rifle into action," said Sam.

Everyone wore Levis blue jeans and flannel shirts.

"The deer can wait," added Bruce.

Summer Mirage

The ground was a faded green with no snow yet.

While driving north, they espied corn to be harvested from the fields yet, and some farmers were out plowing. A yellow Minneapolis-Moline tractor, a red Farmall, and a yellow and green John Deere tractor were seen in the fields.

"I hope we run into a snowstorm up north so we can track the deer better," said Rusty.

"Mind if I turn the dial on the radio?" asked Sam.

"Go ahead and find some music," replied Chester.

Over the airwaves, Eddie Fisher was singing, "Cindy, Oh, Cindy," and the Weavers were performing, "On Top of Old Smokey." The traffic on Highway 52 got heavy as they neared the Twin Cities. Later, the group halted at the Land O' Lakes dairy store in St. Cloud for a lunch and to stretch.

"This looks like a good place to eat," said Rusty.

A lovely girl in a red and white uniform waited on the boys. She had brown hair and was slim looking.

"I am Kay, a college student here, and this is my part-time job."

The hunters ordered northern pike fish and French fries.

"Do you have sports teams at your school?" asked Chester.

"Our college teams are the Huskies. I am interested in architecture and museums," stated Kay.

After the meal, they continued the journey north, passing Brainerd and Cass Lake before entering the town of Bemidji. The first people seen were a few drunken Chippewa Indians staggering around. Chester parked next to the Markham Hotel as the snow started to fall. Many of the brick buildings were built around the year 1900 and later.

"God damn, but it's colder than a witch's tit!" expostulated Sam.

The clock on the Northern National Bank read four degrees Fahrenheit. The farmers from southeastern Minnesota went into the Sweden House and formed a line to select the food they desired. On the side of the room were lined up national flags, including the Scandinavian nations, the USA, Canada, Mexico, and Minnesota. They took their trays into the next room and sat under the chandelier.

"We sure got our money's worth," commented Chester.

"We will have to stop here on our return trip," said Bruce.

Later, they drove past the old brick, county court house and out of town. Snow kept falling as they passed by Red Lake, and it was late at night when the travelers pulled into Warroad. They found a motel and crawled under the warm blankets to rest.

The sunbeams filtered through the snow-covered windows at dawn, and the hunters rolled out of their comfortable beds. A meal of flapjacks, sausages, cereal, and orange juice made all feel robust for a long day in the woods. They made for the forest of jack pine, cedar, and birch trees nearby.

"This looks like a good campsite," said Rusty.

"Hunting and camping go together like a horse and saddle," commented Sammy.

"When did you get brains?" asked his brother, Rusty.

The others chuckled at the humor.

"We are an unique group," said Chester.

They dragged out the tent, stakes, and sleeping bags after parking the car. Then the foursome cleared away some ground and soon had the tent set up and the equipment inside.

"One of us should stay here while the others hunt," said Chester, while taking his rifle out of its case.

"I will stay first," put in Sam.

"Good, I will come back in an hour; we all can take turns," replied Chester.

Rusty, as usual, came up with a good idea. "Let's each walk in separate directions and then return straight towards camp. If there are any deer around, we will drive them towards Sam here in the clearing."

"Okay, let's make it," said Bruce while putting his cap on.

They walked off into the big wilderness separately, each wearing orange or red-colored clothes and carrying a rifle. A gray squirrel was seen gathering nuts and storing them.

The ground was level as Chester sat down on a tree stump to rest. There were a few inches of snow on the ground, and most of the leaves had fallen. Then he espied a timber wolf running fast.

The wolf took one glance at Chester who was standing still as a wooden Indian in a cigar store. He continued walking and saw lone deer tracks a mile out of camp. Chester made an about face and then

Summer Mirage

heard two shots a short distance from camp. He rushed back to where Sam was and saw both brothers standing over a big buck deer.

"Who got him?" inquired Chester.

"I bored him!" replied Sammy.

Rusty and Sam were dressing out the carcass when Bruce came back.

"Did you see anything?" asked Chester.

"I saw three deer, but they were too far away for me to shoot at."

They all ate some lunch; then three walked out again into the north woods while Chester stayed behind in camp. He retired to his car to warm up for a while and read a Straight Arrow comic book and then another dime Indian Chief book.

Then he sat near the tent with his rifle ready for action. After an hour, he heard a noise back in the woods. Something was running, and twigs were snapping under its feet. A huge deer emerged into the clearing and stopped. He aimed his new Winchester and squeezed the trigger, dropping the buck in its tracks. The deer's hind legs were still kicking.

Bruce came on the run singing out, "Did you get one?"

"Yep, we will have plenty of venison to eat this winter," replied Chester.

"Boy, what a honey!" Bruce added.

The two were cutting up the deer when the brothers came stomping back into camp.

"We heard the rifle report," said Rusty.

"God damn, it's cold out, and I have had enough for today!" said Rusty.

"We all put in a full day's work," added Bruce.

The hunters then gathered firewood for a campfire. They remembered that summer vacation when they had gone camping, swimming, and horseback riding at Rusty and Sam's farm. Once again they were camping next to a blazing campfire roasting wieners and marshmallows. The fire cast weird shadows onto the forest.

"Have you heard anything about Bernie Baker lately?" asked Rusty.

"They let him out of the Rochester Nut House last week," replied Chester. "I heard he went to visit his sister on a farm near Ettrick, Wisconsin."

"Gosh, he was in there for pudner a year then!" said Sam.

"Those wieners look done," spoke up Bruce, while he poured cups of hot chocolate. Two deer hung from trees. They had not seen any other hunters in the area.

The teenagers then sat back to relax and reminisce about their recent years and laugh at a few jokes. After a while, they zipped themselves up into their cozy sleeping bags. The campfire was dying down as Rusty lay next to Chester.

"How is the girl Tamra?" he asked.

"She is okay and has plans for attending college in Bemidji later on," replied Chester.

"When do you start?" asked the redhead.

"It might be a while yet because it takes time to save up money."

Outside, the wind died down as a wolf howled off in a distance. The sleeping bags and air mattresses were comfortable, and everyone got a good night's rest. The scene was tranquil.

At dawn, the boys awakened to a voice outside the tent.

"Hey! Is anybody home there?" a man asked.

Chester opened the zipper on his sleeping bag and nudged Sam. The flaps on the tan-colored tent were opened, and Chester peered out to see who the stranger was.

"I am glad to see you boys here because I am almost frozen and lost!" said Bernie Baker.

"Were you deer hunting?" queried Chester.

"Hell, yes, I was with a party of five men and became lost."

Chester started up his car to put the heater on as Bernie got in to warm up. The others began making a fire for breakfast.

"I am surprised to see you here in Paul Bunyon land," said Chester while rolling his window down some.

"A farmer down by Harmony hired me, and he let me off work for a few days to go deer hunting," admitted Bernie. "Our party got two deer yesterday."

Summer Mirage

"We got two also," said Chester.

"Why don't you drive me out to the main road so I can get my bearings, and I should be able to find my party then."

The duo drove a couple of miles within the softwood forest before Bernie said, "I know where I am now."

They came to his camp, and Chester parked his car.

"Here is a can of cold Miller High Life beer," said Bernie upon taking leave.

Chester then returned to his friends who were having breakfast.

"Have some bacon and eggs," said Sam.

"It smells good! Bernie found his outfit," said Chester.

"I will stay in camp first today," stated Rusty.

After eating, the trio started out again separately, and the sun was shining. Chester located wolf tracks near the camp.

As he was walking along, a flock of grouse rose up from a bush and flew away. Then, by a large Norway pine tree stood a gray timber wolf. Since there was a bounty on them, Chester fired his gun. The wolf fell at the first shot, and he picked it up and dragged it towards camp. Upon hearing four shots, he moved towards the direction of the sound.

Chester espied something red standing in the snow. It was the ladies' man, Bruce, looking over the buck he had just bagged.

"That is the biggest deer we got so far!" said Chester upon approaching him.

"He was running when I started shooting my Marlin repeater, and I hit him twice," boasted Bruce.

The two pals dressed out the animal and dragged it into camp one hundred yards away. Sam and Rusty greeted them in jubilation.

"Look at those lucky guys coming!" said Rusty.

They had a campfire going, and all warmed their hands and feet.

"Let me stay in camp again so I will have a better chance to bag a deer," suggested Rusty.

"That's all right with me," said Bruce.

The trio went out into the wilderness again as Rusty stayed behind, hoping that they would chase back a deer for him to bag.

Chester was about a mile out when he came upon a hill. He climbed to the summit and sat down to drink his can of Miller High Life beer. After he started for camp, he came upon two strangers; the lady had blonde hair.

"Hello, Mr. Hunter!" she called out.

"Hello, there!" replied Chester.

Both were sitting on a log and drinking tea from a jug.

"Care for a cup of tea?" asked the man who resembled an athlete.

"Sure, I need something to warm me up," replied Chester.

The man looked at her and winked, knowing that there were two meanings to that answer.

"Did you have any luck yet?" queried Chester.

"No, I saw a deer, but it was too far away to shoot at," said Joe. He looked familiar.

"Do you want some more tea, Marilyn?" he inquired.

"I will take a half cup," replied the lovely lady.

"Where are you from?" she asked.

"From southeastern Minnesota."

"How superb the scenery is down there," she commented.

"Where are you folks from?" asked Chester.

"California. I am an actress in the movies." She then took off her sunglasses and removed a cap that had covered most of her blonde hair.

The teen looked them both over. Suddenly, Chester recognized the famous actress who just happened to be on vacation in the north woods. He took out his address book and pen.

"May I have your autograph?"

"Why sure, anything for a handsome Norwegian-American like you," she replied. "Now you can do me the same favor by signing your autograph," said Marilyn.

"Anything for an interesting California lady," said Chester.

She pulled out a fancy autograph book for Chester to sign.

"Why did you change your name from Norma Jean Baker to Marilyn Monroe?"

"Many movie people do that, including John Wayne and Roy Rogers," she said.

Summer Mirage

"Do you plan on making any more westerns?" asked Chester.

"I will do one in Nevada called "The Misfits", with Clark Gable," Marilyn said.

"I will be sure to see it in a theater."

The trio talked some more before Chester returned to his camp. His three friends were there, and Rusty looked happy.

"Guess what I got? Look here!" he said. Laid out on the ground near the bushes was a buck deer. "I got it on two shots," said Rusty with a sense of pride.

It was late in the afternoon, and they sat around the blazing red campfire. The roasted venison, biscuits, apples, and root beer became an excellent meal. They sat watching the amber coals glow. It was all dark and quiet in the vicinity.

Chester imagined he saw two faces in the glow of the fire, Tamra and Marilyn, both actresses. One was an auburn- haired damsel, and the other a blonde. Which one was prettier? Just then, a timber wolf howled off in the forest.

"Hey! Why don't we go fishing tomorrow now that we have taken our limit of deer?" suggested Rusty.

They laughed, and Sam said, "We are really having fun!"

As the fire died down, the boys retired to the tent and closed the flaps. A call of a moose was heard during the night.

Rusty was the first one up at dawn, and he put wood on the fire to roast venison. Chester made pancakes on a kettle while Sam and Bruce took down the tent. Soon, all were seated around the rustic campfire like four Indian braves, eating breakfast.

Later, they dropped off the four deer at a meat locker by the road for processing; it would be picked up later.

"Lake of the Woods is close by; we can fish there this morning," said Chester.

Before long, the foursome entered the town of Warroad and drove up to the shore of the lake. Steam was coming off the surface because the water was warmer than the air. The lake would freeze over in a few more weeks.

"We can fish from the shore," said Bruce.

There were two fishing rods in the car trunk, and the boys took turns fishing.

After a couple of hours, they had taken four northern pike and five walleyed pike with live bait on the hooks. They then cleaned the fish and put them on ice before starting the homeward journey south. The group spent the night in Bemidji, the village named after a Chippewa Indian Chief.

They stopped at the Chief Motel to spend the night and saw a large mural of an Indian Chief outside. After leaving some items in the room, they went downtown. Near the shore of Lake Bemidji were seen the statues of Paul Bunyon and Babe, the blue ox. They espied the lights on the marquee of the Chief Theater that read: River of No Return.

"Let's go to the show," said Sammy.

"Good, a western starring Marilyn Monroe, Robert Mitchem, and Rory Calhoun," declared Rusty.

The teenagers attended the first showing of the night. Later, they drank root beer at a classy place called the Gastaus, where an old German had started a restaurant.

"I liked the part where Marilyn and Bob Mitchem are on the raft being chased by Indians," said Rusty.

"And the part where she sings the title song in a saloon," added Chester.

Bruce put a quarter in the Wurlitzer jukebox, and Marilyn sang "The River of No Return" and then "Diamonds are a Girl's Best Friend." They finished the pitcher of root beer and returned to the motel.

The next morning, they stopped at the Highway Host truck stop for breakfast and were served the biggest pancakes they had ever seen. They sat next to rugged cigarette-smoking truckers.

Bruce suggested, "Let's stop at the Greenwood Memorial Park because one of my aunts is buried there."

"I always call those places Boothill," said Chester.

Bruce found the resting place of his late aunt, who had been a school teacher in Bemidji. Off to a side, near a dirt path and carved into a tall, granite stone on a different plot of ground, they espied the

Summer Mirage

finest poem they had ever seen. Pearl A. Flint 1885 -- 1905She was both fair and lovely,

But not too good to die.

For the Lord wants all such as her,

To decorate His throne on high.

Pearl's resting place was not far from Bruce's aunt's. Yes, Pearl had been a stranger to them, but what had she looked like, and what had she died from? And at only age twenty. A lot of people had died from tuberculosis and the flu during those early years on the frontier.

An interesting story lies behind every tombstone, so it seems.

The boys made it back to their farms by sunset that day. It had been a happy vacation and hunting trip. The venison and fish would last for weeks to come. The vacation experience changed each person a little bit.

Chapter Sixteen

Bernie and Cliff were chasing cows into the barn on the Jones farm near the hamlet of Harmony, Minnesota. Cliff was a stalwart man, graying at the temples. The sun had become low in the sky. He was standing next to the barn door when suddenly the huge Holstein bull unexpectedly knocked him up against the wall and crushed his chest.

Bernie was standing some distance away. "Son-of-a-bitch, the shitting bull just killed my boss! Now I have to do all the milking and chores myself!" ejaculated Bernie.

Agnes espied Bernie dragging Cliff towards the house, and she screamed.

"What happened to my husband?"

"The bull got ornery and sent Cliff into rosy heaven by bouncing him up against the barn wall!"

Agnes was surprised, "God damn it, now I have to waste about five hundred dollars of hard-earned money on a tear-jerking funeral!"

They dragged the corpse into the house.

Two days later, Bernie and Agnes entered a church at Harmony with the brown casket bearing Cliff. The preacher was in a black robe, and there was a small crowd since it was a working day. There were wooden rows of seats.

The man of God gave his sermon: "Cliff Jones was a good peaceable farmer and is now in farmers' heaven, and his mad bull is on his way to a supermarket. Amen!"

Some days had gone by, and Agnes and Bernie were on a road in her green 1954 Studebaker car. Agnes had auburn hair and hazel eyes and was an attractive lady in her thirties. Now fearing loneliness in the country, she had more interest in Bernie, who was not the best-looking man. She was at the steering wheel of her car.

"I heard that you was a heavy beer drinker, Bernie."

"Oh, hell, yes, but I have been trying to keep the cork on the bottle lately."

He was in a blue suit, and Agnes wore a navy blue outfit with a white sweater.

"I like you, but if you want to make hay with me, you will have to join the Alcoholics Anonymous," she said.

"This is a surprise! Give me their phone number," replied Bernie.

"Better yet, I will take you to their meeting tonight. I once had a drinking problem too."

That night, they parked next to the city hall in Harmony where the meeting was. Then there were a dozen men and women seated facing Bernie who was about to speak.

"I have been to hell and back, and I want to stay sober. Bartenders have taken my money, and I was in a car wreck with a lady friend. I have been in jail and have lost a job because of drinking alcohol. Maybe talking about my past troubles here in public will help."

As Bernie walked to sit down, the others in attendance clapped their hands. The group then had a snack of lemonade and cookies.

"Who was your lady friend in the wreck?" a man asked.

"Sally, who is in Boothill with her soul in heaven," said Bernie.

The strange group then played "500" at cards.

Before long, it was late spring, and heavy snow was falling as Chester Borseth, Bruce Thompson, and Rusty and Sam Wampuch emerged from a blue Chevy in front of the bowling alley in Lewiston. The red-headed and freckle-faced brothers had been close, and Rusty usually had the best ideas. Sam was smarter than he pretended to be and was two years younger in age.

"Let's bowl a set of three games with the loser of the first game buying soda pop," said Chester.

"Fair enough, I need some exercise," put in Bruce. The latter, being the oldest and a ladies' man, always had nice clothes on in public, and he combed his brown hair a lot.

Chester had a purple ball; Bruce owned a golden one; Rusty threw a blue ball, and Sam heaved his green bowling ball.

"I want to bowl my first two-hundred game today!" said Rusty.

Probably the wisest of the group was Chester, the teen who was the second oldest of the foursome.

"Look at Rusty getting a triple; he is on his way to a two-hundred game," said Bruce.

A stranger, Dale Brown, approached them carrying a bottle of Seven-Up. He had dark hair, with a mustache and was of average build. He was intense and unsmiling.

"I remember seeing you boys one day at the trial for Bernie Baker," said Dale.

"Who are you?" asked Chester, while setting down his ball.

"I am Dale Brown, brother of Steve who was shot by Bernie."

"Do you think that Bernie got off too easy?" asked Chester.

"It was his clever defense lawyer who got Bernie off. So where is that hired man now?"

"Bernie is working for Agnes Jones near Harmony. Her husband, Cliff, just got killed by a mad bull," stated Chester.

"Well, the bull smashed the wrong man. It should have been Bernie," retorted Dale. He sauntered away with a frown on his face.

It was May, and Agnes was raking the leaves on their large lawn next to oak and elm trees. Bernie was forking calf manure into a John Deere manure spreader with a five-tine pitchfork. The dog on the farm was Venus, a collie. Suddenly, she barked.

"What is it, Venus?" asked Bernie.

Venus then raced for the pasture where a badger was trying to reach its hole. The dog intercepted it, and a fierce fight developed.

Summer Mirage

"If I only had a camera handy, I could take pictures of the fight," said Bernie.

The struggle only lasted a few minutes, and Venus won but had blood on her. She was limping as the collie and new man approached Agnes near the house.

"I heard some barking; what is it?" she asked.

"Venus is the hero of the day, the survivor of mortal combat," replied Bernie. Now that Bernie was laying off the booze, he was showing a hint of intelligence and was becoming more normal; however, his midwestern vernacular and way of speaking remained the same.

"I am happy we are country folks because we would not have this kind of excitement living in a big, dirty city crowded with people who keep their doors locked," said Agnes.

"I never thought of it that way, but I agree. Growing up on a farm or ranch is the best life possible," added Bernie.

"I don't want any more bulls stalking around here," said Agnes. "From now on, we will use artificial breeding for the dairy herd."

"A good idea," said Bernie while holding his hat.

Dale Brown was sneaking around the house of Agnes in a suspicious manner. He talked in a monologue, "My plan is to scare the daylights out of Bernie, maybe drive him crazy and send him back to the nut house where he belongs. I am not forgetting that he sent my brother Steve to Boothill. He died with his boots on and a lead slug in his chest."

Dale peeked into a window and saw Bernie and Agnes close together and laughing. Bernie then walked alone into the next room. Dale put on a Frankenstein mask and pounded on the rear window, and Bernie saw it waving to him.

"Holy Jesus, that looks like something from a Boris Karloff movie. Agnes, come here quick!"

"What is it, Bernie?"

"I just saw Frankenstein!" he exclaimed.

"Ha, ha, ha, you foolish man!" she replied.

They both looked out the window but saw nothing. Sometime later, they went to bed together just as if they were already married.

"My late father would have disinherited me if he knew that I was sleeping with a man out of wedlock," said Agnes.

"Do you think the cavemen, our ancestors of thousands of years ago, bothered with a silly marriage ceremony?" expostulated Bernie.

The couple were lying in bed under a sheet.

"When a cave man wanted a woman, he just grabbed her by the hair and took her to his cave, sometimes knocking her on the head with a club if she resisted," he explained.

"Ha, ha, ha, you say the funniest things, and that is what I like about you, Bernie."

The next day, Dale Brown was prowling about the farm yard unseen. He talked in a soliloquy.

"If I cannot drive Bernie crazy or scare him to death, maybe I can cause him to have an accident so he can join my brother Steve in Boothill."

Dale entered the farm garage and loosened the nuts on a front wheel of Bernie's brown 1952 Nash car.

Cassandra, the daughter of Agnes, was riding a bicycle carrying the mail from the mailbox at the end of the driveway. She had brown hair and was pretty.

"Here is a postcard for Bernie," she said.

He grabbed the card and read it. "It is from Leslie and Alice Grey; they are on vacation at the Grand Canyon of Arizona. They went on a mule train ride there!"

Agnes looked at the colorful card. "Let's make reservations for a mule train ride too!" she suggested.

"Right now, I need to drive to town for a few supplies," said Bernie.

"May I come along?" asked Cassandra.

"Why sure, honey, I will buy you an ice cream cone," Bernie said.

The pre-teen girl and hired man entered his car and drove down the gravel road. It was late spring, and the corn and oats were up in the fields, all green yet. A blue sky loomed above with big white, fluffy clouds.

"I cannot decide if I like this brown Nash or Mother's green Studebaker car best," said the cute girl.

"As Les Grey once said, they are all made to run," replied Bernie.

As they were slowing down for a stop sign, the right wheel fell off, and the car slid off the road into a level ditch. The girl held on to her seat.

"God damn it, the shits. I'm sober and still end up in a ditch!" expostulated Bernie.

"Oh, don't talk like a dink, Bernie; I don't like that kind of language," retorted Cassandra.

"It's just that I get so frustrated sometimes; I am sorry, honey. Bad luck just happens to me."

Bernie jacked up his car and put the wheel and tire back on. They then went shopping in Harmony village.

That night, Chester and Rusty decided to pay a visit to Bernie to see how he was doing. They parked outside the dirt driveway and walked towards the house when they espied Dale.

"What are you doing here?" queried Chester.

"I want to play a joke on Bernie with a Wolfman mask I am holding here," said Dale.

"I'd like to see Bernie get the shit scared out of him," said Rusty. He would occasionally use a vulgar word.

"Then join me; here are Frankenstein and Dracula masks. Put them on, and we will surprise Bernie outside the barn windows," suggested Dale Brown.

Inside the barn, Bernie was busy milking the cows using Surge buckets. Suddenly, he heard pounding on the windows. He went to peer out a window when Dracula (Chester) appeared. The hired man was frightened.

"Holy fart suckers, it's Dracula come here to the North Star state of Minnesota from the hills of old Transylvania in Romania!" ejaculated Bernie.

He went to another window, and Frankenstein's monster, (Rusty) was seen. Bernie became more afraid when a third window had pounding on it. He moved towards the new commotion.

Carrol P. Peterson

"It's the Wolfman, and the moon is full!" he said. "The Wolfman, Frankenstein, and Dracula have joined forces to get my blood. I have to attack first to survive!"

Bernie grabbed a three-tine hay fork and rushed out to come upon the Wolfman (Dale) first. He drove the pitchfork into the rear end of the monster.

"Ahhh, he got me in the ass...I'm losing my mind!" ejaculated Dale.

The other two youths in disguises were too fast for the hostile Bernie and ran off into the darkness. Dale also escaped. Then Agnes came out of her house.

"What is all the commotion about? Why are you holding a pitchfork, Bernie?" she asked.

"Frankenstein, Dracula, and the Wolfman came after me on this night of the full moon. I just poked the Wolfman in the ass, and he squealed like a stuck pig!" stated Bernie.

Agnes went into a laughing fit over the unbelievable man. They were both in blue jeans standing in the moonlight.

"That is the funniest story I have heard all year. Not even Bob Hope or Red Skeleton ever came up with a story like that! I got a joker for a hired man!" exclaimed Agnes.

Bernie stood there like a wooden Indian in a cigar store, speechless. He then returned to the barn.

Rusty and Chester reached the latter's dark blue Chevy.

"Did you see Dale get poked in his hinder by Bernie's hay fork?" asked Rusty.

"Yep, he will have a tough time on his trips to the bathroom for a while," replied Chester.

"Farmers rarely use the bathroom anyway because they are outside most of the time," returned Rusty.

They shared a laugh.

"We are still having a good time, aren't we," added the redhead.

"That is what we are on Earth for, to laugh and have a good time," said smart Chester with his subtle wisdom.

Dale had stopped in the darkness of the woods where he escaped. He talked in a monologue. "Nothing has worked, and I have tried to scare Bernie or drive him crazy. Then I caused him to have an accident when his car wheel fell off. For all my efforts, I have only three extra holes in my God damn ass!"

Meanwhile, Tamra Hunt, the auburn-haired beauty, was out pushing a lawn mower in late spring; she was wearing yellow shorts and trying to get a suntan. Her mother, June, an older version of Tamra, rushed outside.

"There is a telephone call for you, Tamra!" she shouted.

The girl, now on school vacation, rushed inside the house. "Hello, it's me, the farmer's daughter!" greeted Tamra.

"There is a picnic at the Archess Park on Sunday, can you come?" asked Chester.

"Oh, hell yes, I'd love to come if you pick me up, you farm boy!"

"Ha, ha, ha, now you are talking like that goofy Bernie Baker. I will pick you up at noon on Sunday in my blue Chevrolet."

Sunday dawned a beautiful day as Tamra and Chester emerged from his car. They saw Molly Olson, a brown-haired girl with Rusty. Bruce Thompson, with a new girlfriend, also appeared at the park in the valley, called the Archess.

"Hello, friends. Meet my girlfriend, April Christmas," said Bruce.

"Hello, I thought Christmas was in December," replied Tamra.

"That is what everyone says," returned April.

She had green eyes and auburn hair and was almost as tall as Bruce. She had on green shorts and a yellow blouse.

There were bluffs of oak and elm trees with a creek running by the park like a picture postcard scene.

"I wonder where Sam is?" asked Molly.

"He is over by the brook to see if any fish are there. He is coming now," said Rusty.

"Did you see any fish, Sam?" asked Chester.

"Yep, but we are not fishing today. A baseball game is planned for after lunch."

The question was which one the three young ladies was the most attractive? Molly, the brown-haired beauty, or Tamra or April, the two auburn-haired girls? None was shorter than five feet, six inches tall;

all were above average in intellect, and all had different life plans and experiences.

The seven people partook of a wiener and marshmallow roast. All were having a good day in the country.

"Molly and I have been comparing each other in relation to our skills. She is the best cook and knows a lot of delicious recipes," stated Tamra.

"Tamra is the best scholar and has read the most books," said Molly.

"And April is the best cowgirl; you should see her ride my white horse, Silver," added Bruce.

"When are you going to get a girlfriend, Sam?" asked April.

He blushed some before answering. "I am in no hurry until I finish high school. It costs money to go on dates."

The four males of early manhood and the three young ladies ran out onto the baseball diamond to play.

All soon changed places of batting, pitching, and fielding. Chester, the best pitcher, struck out Sam and Bruce on curve balls and change-ups.

"You can try out for a minor league team, Chester, since you really got some sneaky pitches," ejaculated Bruce.

"I do not think I'd like all the traveling around to the different cities. The bus, train, or airplane might crash, and I would not live any longer than a horse or a cow on the farm," smartly answered Chester.

"I don't know about you, my friend; you make a speech out of a simple answer," retorted Bruce.

The group had a laugh out of that and all were happy.

"It's just that Chester has a big brain for a farm boy, and we all trust him anyway," added Rusty.

They ended the baseball game and left the park in cars; all were wearing sunglasses. The golden sunbeams filtered through the trees upon the denizens of the park enjoying those lazy, hazy days of summer. A century or two ago, there might have been Indian teepees there instead of picnic tables.

Times change, so it seems.

Summer Mirage

"I wish there were some girls' softball teams around here this summer," said Tamra as she rode in the front seat next to her male friend.

"Maybe there will be some teams next year," said Chester.

From the car radio emanated the tunes of "Blue Tango" by LeRoy Anderson, and "I Just Go Nuts At Christmas" by Yogi Yorgasen; they were played for all those people who would get killed on the roads before the holidays.

Chapter Seventeen

A couple of weeks passed by, and it was haying time on the Borseth farm. A procession of farm vehicles was moving up the farm driveway. Les Grey was steering a green Oliver tractor and pulling an orange Allis Chalmars forage blower, and Ole, with a middle-aged bulge, was driving a John Deere tractor and pulling a red Gehl harvester with a green wagon behind. Chester was driving a smaller green and yellow tractor and pulling a second hay wagon. The dog, Adolf, was trotting along close by. The men dismounted to talk.

"I always liked the smell of cut hay drying in summer," said Ole.

"The city folks miss out on the smells and sounds of farm life," added Lester.

Lucy, wife of Ole, still had dark hair and had said that she had read every book in her small town library. She emerged from her house. "It's past noon and I got steak, corn on the cob, potatoes, and apple pie on the table."

"You heard my wife; let's grab some grub!" said Ole.

The family sat down to eat.

Louie was on the heavier side, resembling Ole. Louie was something like Rusty in that he came up with good ideas. "I found a way to catch more pocket gophers with my death clutch traps!"

"Well, tell us about it, Louie," said Les.

"I smoke the traps a few times a month to get rid of the odors," said the trapper.

Summer Mirage

"Fantastic, I will have to try that!" said Les.

He sometimes said things too close for comfort.

"Tell me, Lucy, how did you happen to marry this fat man, Ole here?" asked Les.

She laughed a little. "Ole was not fat when I married him. I guess I am too good a cook since he gobbles up everything I put on the table, just like the fat turkeys gobble up corn and oats on the ground," explained Lucy.

"Ha, ha, ha, now she compares me to turkeys!" ejaculated Ole.

"I could have married a smart lawyer from Preston, but I guess I like the farm life better," returned Lucy.

"You made the right choice by marrying a dumb farmer like me," retorted Ole.

They all had a hearty laugh.

As they walked outdoors, thunder and lightning occurred in the sky, and rain fell.

"When it rains, farmers go to town," said Les. Chester, Les, and Ole got into Les' brown 1953 Oldsmobile.

"We need a few things at the Gambles store in Lewiston," said Ole.

After buying the items needed, they parked in front of the White Knight Tavern. They entered the bar, and Ole addressed the pretty blonde girl, July.

"Two bottles of Bub's beer."

"What will you have, handsome?" she inquired of Chester.

"A Royal Crown Cola and a snickers candy bar."

A Seeberg jukebox was playing the song, "Why Don't You Believe Me" by Joni James, with her unique singing style. A farmer of Scottish descent had a goofy laugh, like a dying sheep.

"Look who just walked in; it's Bernie Baker and a lady," said Chester.

He and Les walked over to the couple.

"Speak of the devil! Howdy, Les!" said Bernie.

"You God damn old fart sucker," answered Les with a laugh.

The group had a laugh while Les shook hands with his former hired man.

"Meet my new boss, Agnes Jones of Harmony," said Bernie.

"Hello, Agnes, I am glad to meet you," offered Les.

"Hi, I bet you could tell me a lot about my hired man," she replied. She wore orange slacks and a brown blouse.

"More than you want to hear," said Les with a laugh.

The group talked and socialized while tractors entered a feed mill nearby. Some drinkers smoked cigarettes.

A golden sunrise dawned as Dale Brown was sneaking up to a barn on the Jones' farm. He weakened a rope by cutting it almost through and laid it by a blower pipe.

Bernie later left the house and came to the blower machine and started pulling on the rope connected to the pipe, raising it to the barn door above.

"I wonder if Agnes and I are going to do all the haying work ourselves?" he uttered.

The orange-colored pipe was half way up the side of the red barn when the rope broke, and the heavy pipe fell upon Bernie.

"Oh, I'm hurt," he said.

Just then, Agnes espied Dale running from the corner of the machine shed to the woods. She rushed to the aid of Bernie.

"Are you okay? Have any broken bones or pain?"

"I hope not, but I am badly bruised, and the pipe just missed my head!" he replied.

"I saw Dale running off to the woods. Let's inspect this rope," suggested Agnes.

"Look, it's been cut mostly through!" he ejaculated.

"Here on the ground is a pocket knife with the initials DB," said Agnes. "I will call the fat sheriff."

Within an hour, the brown 1954 Chrysler halted at Dale Brown's simple cabin in a woods. George, with his beer belly or Milwaukee front, emerged from his car in a brown uniform, and Dale was on foot nearby.

"Is this your pocket knife, Mr. Brown?" he asked.

"Hell, yeah, so what?" said Dale.

"This was used to cause an accident at the Agnes Jones farm this morning," stated the human bull.

"You are full of Duroc pig shit, fat boy!" firmly expostulated Dale.

The sheriff grabbed Dale by the hair and dragged him to the ground and forced handcuffs on him. "I will show you who is the boss here! I am taking you to the county jailhouse!" exclaimed George.

The sunset loomed gold and purple with a silver lining over the fields of corn and woods as Bernie and Agnes sat on a porch. He was still bruised with a bandage on an arm. The collie, Venus, was lying nearby.

"You could have gotten killed today, Bernie," said Agnes.

"The Alcoholics Anonymous has helped me stay sober, so how about you and I go to town and get hitched?" he asked.

"We belong to different churches, so maybe a Justice of the Peace would be appropriate," suggested Agnes. "I see that you are a strong man, and that is what I need here on the farm."

"I am not the best-looking man around, but you must see something in me that you like, and I adore your auburn hair and hazel eyes," confessed Bernie.

Agnes was a free-spirited lady and smart enough to make good decisions. Bernie had been kind of unpredictable, but seemed to be on the right track. In a short time they were at the Justice of the Peace's house and stood before a gray-haired man.

He concluded with, "I marry you both as man and wife. Do you have a wedding ring?" asked the old fart.

"Oh, hell, yes. Here it is!" said the groom. Bernie put the diamond ring on the finger of Agnes.

The couple then left for a wedding trip out West.

Back at the Borseth farm, Rusty, Molly, Bruce, April, Chester, and Tamra were standing next to Chester's blue 1952 Chevy. The weather was perfect with a sunny sky.

"Like singer Dinah Shore said on her musical television program, 'See the USA in your Chevrolet,' this will be another summer vacation we will never forget, a road trip to the Grand Canyon of Arizona," said Chester.

"Why are your brothers Louie and Sam not coming along?" asked April.

"They need to help with the farm work, but they will get their chance later for a vacation," replied Rusty.

"We can all change off driving the Chevy," suggested Bruce.

The six young people stepped into the car and made a trail of dust down the gravel road. Hours later, they were at the Badlands Park in South Dakota. They got out to stretch and see the scenery.

"My goodness, what a desolate landscape!" exclaimed Tamra.

"It's no good for farming," added Chester.

Later, they arrived at the Mount Rushmore National Historic Site of the four faces of Presidents as the rocky and wooded hills changed color with the gold and lilac dusk. The six-some parked and walked closer.

"How did they carve up those boulders without falling down?" asked Bruce.

"You don't know, do you!" replied Rusty in jest.

"This is a public history lesson! The faces of Jefferson, Washington, Lincoln, and Teddy Roosevelt on stone!" said Tamra.

The next day, the group was nearing the Rocky Mountains in the car.

"We should have taken a different route because it's really scary climbing Summit Mountain!" said Molly.

The girls were afraid.

"It's a lot different being here in person than seeing the mountains in pictures!" added April.

"Hey, gang, do you know who my girlfriend April resembles?" asked Bruce.

"Yep, she looks a lot like actress Mary Murphy in the movie, "The Wild One", with Marlon Brando and the movie, "The Maverick Queen", starring with Jim Davis," answered Molly.

"Thanks! What a good compliment," replied April.

Summer Mirage

"Molly resembles Pier Angeli in the movie, "Somebody Up There Likes Me", starring with Paul Newman," said Rusty.

"And Tamra resembles Marilyn Monroe in the movie, "Asphalt Jungle," put in Chester. "That's a 1950 movie."

"I am glad we are traveling by car so we can see the land better," stated Rusty.

"You don't see much from a fast airplane," added Tamra.

Two days passed before the group came to the Mesa Verde Cliff Dwellings. The three couples climbed up a hill by foot to see the ancient Indian historic homes.

"What state are we in now?" asked Molly.

"We are in southwestern Colorado, and the best scenery in America is right here in the golden West," said Chester.

"I can't argue that; this is tremendous!" said Molly.

The travelers spent hours at the park exploring.

Late the following day, the vacationers reached the rim of the Grand Canyon and observed a spectacular sunset as the canyon changed colors.

"My God, looking down into those one-mile depths is scarier than being up in the Rocky Mountains!" stated Tamra.

They spent a few minutes in stark silence just looking at the chasm.

"It is beautiful," said April. She wore a red shirt.

"We can stay at the lodge tonight and go on the mule train ride tomorrow morning," said Chester.

"Look over there; it's the Watchtower!" said Rusty.

They walked to the lodge for supper.

At dawn, the sun was peeking over the rim of the canyon as Molly, Tamra, April, Chester, Bruce, and Rusty climbed onto the gray mules for a ride down the Bright Angel trail in the Grand Canyon.

"This is the ride of a lifetime!" said Rusty.

"Just think, it took the Colorado River millions of years to carve this gorge!" exclaimed Chester.

"Hey, friends, I have it figured out who our male friends resemble," said Tamra. "Chester resembles Randolf Scott in the movie, "Fort Worth", 1951, while Rusty looks like Joel McCrea in the 1939 movie, "Union Pacific", and Bruce resembles Gary Cooper in the 1940 movie, "The Westerner"."

The guide was a male Hopi Indian wearing his native clothes; he was named Purple Cloud. "An interesting fact is that western author, Zane Grey of Ohio, roped mountain lions here in 1907," said Purple Cloud.

The adventurers descended into the slopes as they reached Phantom Ranch. Upon dismounting for refreshments, they came upon two familiar faces.

"I don't believe it! There is Bernie Baker with a lady; they're drinking coffee and eating lunch!" ejaculated Rusty.

"I am not drunk, but I believe I see some people from Minnesota!" said Bernie.

"What are you doing here?" asked Rusty.

"I can answer that. Bernie and I just got married, and we drove out here to see the Grand Canyon," said Agnes.

"This is the biggest coincidence of the year; what a tiny world!" said Tamra Hunt.

"I heard what happened to your boss, Cliff, back in the barnyard," put in Bruce.

"That big bull made Agnes a widow, but she has me now; I am the substitute," said Bernie.

"The new substitute!" uttered Rusty.

The whole group got a big laugh.

The mule train continued back up the winding trail as a cougar and several black-tailed deer were seen. An eagle hovered overhead looking for food. All the riders wore cowboy hats.

Back in the upper Midwest, George, the sheriff, was letting Dale Brown out, and he walked free.

"You served your time, but do not go near the Agnes Jones farm." The lawman then emitted a book-slamming fart.

"I hear you, but I'm a peace-loving man," replied Dale.

Summer Mirage

He strolled down the sidewalk in the town of Preston and entered a saloon. Dale talked in a soliloquy, "I have to find a way to get even with Bernie. The fat sheriff kept me in jail for a whole month."

Dale was moody as he watched construction going on.

By autumn, Tamra and Chester were walking to Birch Hall at Bemidji State College; they were carrying suitcases.

"The last time I was in Bemidji was to go on a deer-hunting trip with my friends," said Chester.

"I love those birch and pine trees and the big Lake Bemidji," commented Tamra.

"I wonder how many people have drowned in it?" he asked.

The two friends registered at the desk and departed to opposite wings of the dormitory. A calendar on the wall showed September 1956. That night they went to a movie downtown.

"I am trying out for cheerleader," stated Tamra with a smile. She wore a pink sweater and blue jeans.

"For me, it's trying out for quarterback on the Beaver football team," said Chester.

The western movie at the Chief Theater on Beltrami Avenue was The Maverick Queen with a Wyoming setting.

While seated, Tamra commented, "I like Mary Murphy's hat and clothes."

"The best part is Jonie James singing the title song," said Chester. He wore a blue shirt and Levis jeans.

After the movie, the couple walked up the sidewalk. As he was looking away, someone grabbed Tamra from behind and pulled her away. In seconds, Chester realized he was walking alone.

"Where are you, Tamra?" He then heard a loud scream from the dark alley. He hurried to investigate and saw a Chippewa Indian from the reservation force Tamra into an old Ford truck.

He ran after it, but the truck sped away. Chester saw the license number and wrote it down. He hurried to a police patrol car parked at a corner.

"Help! Two Indians just kidnapped my girlfriend!"

The cops took off with him along, but they lost the truck in traffic. The rough-looking men took Tamra to a cabin in the jack pine forest north of town.

Big Foot was the heavy drinker and swore a lot, while Brave Eagle was the cook who was the smarter one. They wore white man's clothes.

"Let me go; I am only a college girl, and I just arrived in Bemidji," pleaded Tamra.

"We are lonely, and you will keep us company," said Big Foot.

They entered a cabin, and Brave Eagle lighted a lantern with its flickering light. Big Foot had a bottle of blackberry brandy and took a long drink; he then gave the bottle to his partner.

"This is a night to celebrate!" said Brave Eagle.

"It is chilly tonight; give me a swig too," requested Tamra.

"Did you hear that? Our lady wants a drink!" said Big Foot.

She slapped his face. "Don't call me your lady!" Tamra expostulated.

The men found her amusing and laughed. "Tamra has true grit!" said Brave Eagle.

She then slapped his face. Big Foot had a laughing spell, but the other Indian stayed sober.

"Don't worry, girl; we are just lonely Indian bums and like some lady company. Nobody is going to rape you," said Brave Eagle.

"How long are you going to keep me?" she asked.

"Only two days, and we will be happy together," said Brave Eagle.

Tamra then felt relieved at the situation.

That same day, Chester was talking to a policeman in front of Deputy Hall on the college campus.

"Did you find Tamra yet?" asked Chester.

"No, but we searched all the streets for the truck and a license number you gave me. Today, we are going to the forest and look for signs of the kidnapping," replied the cop.

"Here is my telephone number at Birch Hall. Call me as soon as you find her." Chester then attended a class.

Summer Mirage

The sunbeams were filtering through the cabin windows as Tamra was frying eggs and bacon for herself and the two Indians. Brave Eagle was pouring coffee, and Big Foot was putting his boots on. It was cool in the cabin.

"I need to return to college today and attend classes," said Tamra.

"Why didn't you run off last night? The door was unlocked," said Brave Eagle.

"This is the north woods and close to Canada. There are bear and wolf nearby, and cougars sometimes stray this far east," explained Tamra.

By mid-morning, Brave Eagle was stringing a guitar.

"Can you play this guitar and sing a song for us?"

"Yeah, if you promise to let me go and drive me back to college at noon today," said Tammy.

"It's a deal," replied Brave Eagle.

She was given the guitar. Tamra stood while singing the title song from the 1954 color movie, "River of No Return", starring Marilyn Monroe; she played the guitar expertly.

At the end the Indians cheered.

Suddenly, two sheriff's deputies wearing brown uniforms burst into the cabin with guns drawn. One was skinny and the other fat.

"Hands up, you kidnapping redskins!" exclaimed the skinny one.

Tamra screamed and dropped the guitar.

"Don't fire; we are peaceful Indians," ejaculated Brave Eagle.

Tamra recovered her composure and spoke, "It's all right; they were going to drive me back to college in an hour."

The two lawmen seemed confused in that unique situation.

"Tamra spoke the truth; no harm was done," said Big Foot.

"This is hard to believe! A kidnapped girl playing a guitar for her abductors!" said the fat deputy.

"They only had a lonely spell, and I brought some cheer into their sad lives," explained Tamra.

"All right, come with us then, lady," said the skinny cop.

The two uniformed human apes left with Tamra in the brown patrol car. When they arrived at Birch Hall to let Tamra off, the fat cop stepped out of the car and blew rapid-fire, tommy-gun farts. A brisk

Carrol P. Peterson

wind was blowing leaves from the birch trees to the ground, and the sun was out.

From that experience, Tamra learned to be more watchful while walking down a sidewalk at night.

Chapter Eighteen

Chester was in a green and white football uniform taking handoffs and passing during a practice session. Suddenly, Tamra in brown slacks and a green sweater raced onto the field of green grass.

"Here I am, Chester, safe and sound!" Tamra informed him.

"Holy Jesus, tell me what happened to you!" Chester shouted.

"It was only two lonely Chippewa Indians who had drunk too much brandy. They took me to their cabin last night! No harm was done!" stated Tammy.

"What about today? Did you escape?" he queried.

"Two law men came just before they were going to take me back to school. I ended up playing their guitar and singing a song," she said.

"Amazing, but I have to practice football now. I will talk to you later," said Chester. The farm boy then heaved a long pass which was caught.

Later, Tamra and five other pretty girls in green and white skirts and sweaters were practicing cheerleading on the sidelines of the gridiron.

An hour later, Chester was carrying a briefcase, and Tamra held on to a few books as they walked under pine and birch trees near Pine Hall.

"You did not press charges against those two Indians?" he asked, while looking at two squirrels climb trees.

"No, they have a tough enough struggle just to survive."

"Guess what, I will be playing against my friend, Rusty Wampuch, on Saturday when we play against the Winona State Warriors here in the north country," stated Chester.

"There is a dance at the gym afterwards, and I hope that his girlfriend, Molly Olson, is along," commented Tamra.

The Bemidji State College Beavers were playing the Winona State Warriors. Chester emerged from the huddle and then threw a long, completed pass. Rusty made the tackle on the five-yard line, and he and Chester waved to each other.

"Good play, Rusty, a smart move!" he shouted.

"You burned us on the pass!" said Rusty.

Chester then scored a touchdown on a quarterback draw.

Then the Beaver cheerleaders jumped and yelled, "Push them in the lake! Push them in the lake!"

The bleachers were full of students, some cheering, but most were silent. The game was a tie.

That night, there was a lot of youth and beauty in the gym as Molly, Rusty, Chester, and Tamra were in casual clothes and talking. The gym was decorated superbly.

"How is college in Winona?" asked Tamra.

"The instructors are trying to make a scholar out of me. I hear you are studying every day, Tamra," replied Molly.

"That is what college is for, to study and learn about the world," stated Tamra.

Couples were then dancing.

"At Winona, I have observed that those students who sit in the Student Union Smog room all day smoking cigarettes and playing cards and then go out every night to have a good time do not last long. They flunk out of school," explained Rusty.

"You made some good tackles today, Rusty," observed Chester.

"I was satisfied with the twenty-to-twenty tie game," replied the red head.

The live band then played the tune "Tan Shoes and Pink Shoe Laces" by Dodie Stevens. Then a slow cheek-to-cheek tune by Pat Boone, "Love Letters in the Sand," was played.

The two couples only danced to slow tunes because they did not like the rapid-style music when people were jigging around like natives in a jungle.

The following day, Tamra and her pal sat next to each other in class where a man lectured. Henry was a tall and handsome teacher with dark brown hair.

"Wars don't just happen; there is a reason for everything. Remember don't take everything that you read as the gospel truth since there are a lot of bad books being published," he explained.

There were about a dozen students in the class, and all liked the instructor.

That evening, Chester and Tamra were playing a game of chess using her expensive onyx stone set from Mexico.

"You are right; playing chess is like a game of war, and it's a paradox. One can be staring at the board and not see an impending move," Tamra smartly observed.

There was deep concentration on their faces as they moved the pieces slowly.

Two days later on a bright day, Rusty and Chester were using shears to trim Christmas trees on a bright day in a forest. They were busy on balsam fir trees.

"A friend of mine at college is paying us good money to help trim his trees on his tree farm," said Chester.

"This is something different, and I can use the exercise. Did you know Molly looks good while cheer leading in a purple and white uniform?" asked Rusty.

The following Saturday, the football game was at Winona, and Molly was cheering with other girls on the sideline.

"Dam the Beavers! Dam the Beavers!" they shouted.

Chester threw a pass for the BSC Beavers, but the receiver was hit hard and dropped the ball. Rusty, playing for the Warriors picked up the football and ran fifty yards for a touchdown. Molly and the other five purple, gold, and white-clad girls went wild in their frenzy.

Carrol P. Peterson

After the game, Rusty, Molly, Chester, and Tamra went on a walking tour of the 19th century Julius Wilkie steamboat on the Winona riverfront. They stood along the railing overlooking the Mississippi River.

"A lot of gambling and drinking once took place on this old steamboat," said Rusty.

"This is where the famous cliché 'You bet' was first spoken," said Chester.

"You bet I like this steamboat!" exclaimed Molly.

The foursome had a good laugh.

"I am looking forward to our one-week camping trip to Lake of the Woods on the Canadian border," said Tamra.

Some days later, six youths were on their way up north to Warroad, and after reaching the shore, they carried their luggage onto a cruiser. Molly, Tamra, April, Chester, Rusty, and Bruce were soon moving over the big lake that bordered two countries. Many wooded islands were seen en route. Rusty and Bruce had their fishing poles out and were trolling for Northern and Walleyed Pike.

"I am trying out for baseball pitcher when I return to college," said Chester.

"I like to roam the outfield best on the baseball diamond," added the ladies' man, Bruce.

The teenagers were in swimsuits trying to get suntans, and the girls were rubbing suntan lotion on. They were relaxing, and some fish were caught. Meanwhile, the wind increased in speed.

"Look, a storm is brewing in the southwest!" said Bruce.

"That is the most dangerous direction for a storm to come from," commented Chester.

A strong wind developed, and the boat swayed back and forth. The girls became fearful as they clung to the railings and their boyfriends.

"God help us! Don't let this cruiser tip over! This is not the Titanic of 1912!" exclaimed Tamra.

A big wave swept onto all, and the vacationers became soaked with water.

"Help! Help!" screamed Molly and April.

Summer Mirage

They had a fearful time for a spell, but soon arrived at Oak Island and anchored ashore. The lake was stormy as the six-some left the cruiser and made their way to cabins. It was still raining and thundering when the three couples unpacked and sat around the cozy fireplace. Tamra had a guitar and sang the Elvis hit song, "Love Me Tender."

Everyone was singing when the tune was half over. Tammy was the star of the evening.

Outside, a black bear was prowling around the cruiser. The group went to sleep for the night as the amber glow on the wood subsided in the fireplace.

Just after dawn, they had an outdoor meal of fried eggs, toast, bacon, and hot chocolate. The blue smoke curled up over the oak and elm trees from the campfire. Then they embarked in three canoes, pairing off with two persons in each canoe and paddling near the shore of the woods.

"This is really the life! The Indians did this for many centuries and are still enjoying the wilderness with us!" said Bruce.

They all wore hats to protect and shade their heads from the sun even though the temperature was not hot.

"This canoe paddling is getting Molly and me in shape for cheer leading!" stated Tamra.

"Has everyone got their life jackets on tight?" asked the brown-haired Chester.

Heeding his good advice, everyone looked to his or her straps and tightened them.

The vacationers sighted wild animals along the shore that included black bear, deer, moose, beaver, geese, and ducks. The sky was blue with big marshmallow, fluffy clouds. An eagle soared overhead, and they passed by a dam with a beaver perched on top. The lake was a clean blue color.

"Look! A canoe with two paddlers is approaching us!" said April.

Bruce took out his binoculars for a better look. "That form with the dark hair looks familiar! It's Estelle Gill, whom I went on a hayride with months ago! She resembles actress Marsha Hunt in the 1943 color movie, The Human Comedy," exclaimed the observer.

"You mean now I have competition?" asked April.

Estelle was in the canoe with her father, Zane.

Upon coming closer, Estelle greeted the group, "Hello, friends, what a surprise!"

"What brings you to the north woods?" asked Bruce.

"I am here on vacation with my family," replied Estelle.

"I am glad to meet you people," put in Zane. He was average looking and wearing a brown hat.

They all went ashore to talk and get acquainted more.

"You can join our group for the last days of our vacation here if you wish, Estelle," said Chester.

"Is that okay with you, Father?" asked Estelle.

"Why sure, honey. I will paddle back to my wife now," said Zane.

Just before sunset, they strung up a volleyball net, and a game began. They were all having a good time in the sunshine and grass.

"I rather envy Bruce with having two girlfriends here," said Rusty with a smile.

They all had a good laugh.

"April and my other pal Estelle are good players. Watch them serve the ball at the corners," said Bruce.

"This is different from playing volleyball indoors," added Estelle, the brunette.

They soon tired from batting the ball back and forth with their hands.

The seven teenagers gathered around the campfire for a wiener roast. Tamra played her guitar and sang the Four Preps' hit tune, "Twenty-Six Miles" and then Pat Boone's popular song, "April Love." The entire group joined in singing the last song.

"I am happy here, as we all are, but it's also a sad thought knowing that this might be our last vacation on Oak Island together," said April thoughtfully.

"Everyone goes their own way sooner or later," added the wise Chester.

"The time may come when you will have to choose between me and April," said Estelle while looking at Bruce.

"That is a dilemma," he replied.

"I have a solution. Estelle and April can have a horse race, and the winner would win the love of Bruce," suggested Rusty.

The group again laughed even though they knew it was a good idea.

"We accept," said Estelle and April in unison.

"Me three," put in Bruce. "Let's plan for it after the main horse race at the St. Charles fair."

"Maybe Bruce will end up like a Mormon with two wives," said Molly.

The girls were wearing Bermuda shorts and very colorful blouses.

A couple of weeks passed by, and a game of baseball was in progress south of Lake of the Woods in Bemidji. Chester was on the mound for the Beavers doing the pitching. He struck out a batter; then Rusty came to bat for the Warriors.

"Show me your best pitches," he said.

"I only have four, the fast ball, a curve, a change-up, and a sinker," replied Chester.

Rusty swung and missed on the first two pitches; then he slammed a home run to tie the game at four runs each. He ran the bases with a smile, and Molly was in the grandstand cheering.

"My real life-hero from a farm," she exclaimed.

At the end of the game, Rusty and Chester shook hands while wearing opposing uniforms. They were happy playing the great American game. Tamra was seated next to Molly.

In a different part of the state, Bernie and Agnes were on a golf course behind Cady's red barn in Lewiston. It was a bright and sunny day when Dale was watching with binoculars from behind a grove of trees. Agnes wore pink shorts, while Bernie had on blue trousers.

"You can drive the golf ball almost as far as me," said Bernie.

"Exercise on the farm has put me in great shape," replied Agnes. She drove the ball with a good swing, and then they walked together.

"No golf cart for me because I walk the course and carry my own clubs," said Bernie.

He and Agnes rested on a wooden bench and drank water from a canteen.

"Did they let Dale out of jail yet?" asked Agnes.

"Yeah, he is out, and he caused that farm injury when the blower pipe fell on me," replied Bernie.

"Maybe you had better keep a hawk eye on things because Dale may not have learned his lesson yet."

Later in the day, Bernie was driving an Allis Chalmars WD orange-colored tractor pulling a manure spreader. Venus, the golden collie and a good dog, was trotting along.

In the background were fields of green corn, alfalfa, and oats turning gold. Agnes stepped out of her green 1954 Studebaker car and picked a few flowers from her garden.

"These will look good in a vase on the table in the living room," she said. She carried in some marigolds and peonies.

A while later, she was watching Bernie shovel corn into a corn sheller that was run by a tractor and a leather pulley. "I love work because I can stand and watch it for hours," said Agnes.

Bernie put down his shovel. "Ha, ha, ha, you and your clever remarks," replied the hired man.

After the job was finished, she asked, "What would you do if Dale showed up here again?"

"I will have a concealed weapon and send that bastard on a one-way vacation trip to Boothill," responded Bernie.

"Ha, ha, you and your friends from Boothill. You have been watching "Gunsmoke" too much on television," she replied.

A mailman drove up to the mailbox to deliver the mail. Cassandra walked to get the mail while humming Gene Autry's "Back in the Saddle" tune. Ducks were on the pond nearby and quacking.

"I like to read the comic strips," she said.

Chapter Nineteen

The annual event of the rodeo at the Winona County Fair in St. Charles was on hand. In the old wooden grandstand were Les and Alice Grey, Ole and Lucy Borseth, and Tim and Hilda Wampuch. There were bucking horses in the ring.

"That is a tough life, being a rodeo rider, but I imagine they are paid well," commented Alice.

"And they get to see a lot of country," added Lucy. "I like to see those riders in their colorful clothes and saddles."

Soon, riders on horseback were getting set for a race.

"I love races," said Tim.

"Look, there is Chester on his golden palomino, Fury," said Ole.

A bell rang, and a dozen horses were galloping for a grand-prize trophy around the dirt racetrack.

"Rusty is on Tony, his bay horse, and Bruce is on a white horse, Silver, and Sam is on his Sorrel, Wildfire, while Louie is on Dick, his strawberry roan," said Hilda proudly.

The riders whipped their mounts with the leather reins. Rusty took the lead at first, but soon Bruce and Sam got past him. Chester had an inside angle and furiously whipped Fury to more speed. He edged Sam and Bruce at the finish line. His folks stood up and cheered.

"Yippee, Chester is the winner," shouted Lucy.

After the race, the riders walked their horses to cool them off.

"I did not think Fury could beat Silver," said Chester.

Carrol P. Peterson

"Maybe next year, I will get luckier," replied Bruce.

"Maybe Fury had a better breakfast than our horses had," added Rusty.

They all had a good laugh.

"I will have to train Dick better," said Louie.

Molly, Tamra, and April joined their boyfriends as they strolled into the animal exhibit barns to see horses, sheep, pigs, chickens, ducks, and cattle. Estelle had already met the boys earlier. Before long, they were in the midway, and all got on a Ferris wheel.

"Did you know that only a pin holds us up here, Molly?" asked Rusty when they stopped at the zenith.

"Don't scare me like that!" she replied. Molly thought to herself, If the pin breaks, Rusty will save me because he always has good ideas.

People below watched the three couples, and they looked at Bruce the most with his two girlfriends, April and Estelle.

All the young people were laughing while their parents were in the beer garden drinking Bub's and Hamm's beer.

"Don't drink too much beer, Ole; you have to drive home later," said Lucy while they were looking at the western-style beer hall.

The sounds of the people and rides lasted for hours.

The next day was the big race between Estelle and April to see who would win Bruce's favor. Only the seven friends and Sam knew of the race.

Big white cumulus clouds were sailing in the sky with a brisk breeze.

"I will ride Silver because the horse knows me," said April Christmas.

Just then, Sam joined the group leading his mount, Wildfire.

"I now have a choice of three horses, and I think I will try Sam's sorrel," said the brunette, Estelle Gill.

"Rusty is waiting at the big oak tree a quarter mile south of here. Ride to him and back to here. The rider that returns to us first wins the race," said Chester.

"Good luck to you both," said Tamra.

Estelle and April mounted their horses bareheaded and got ready for the whistle. Bruce blew it, and the girls were off with a cloud of dust.

"Let's ride, Wildfire," shouted Estelle.

"Hi ho, Silver," hollered April.

The girls' hair flew with the wind and it was a sight to see them whipping their mounts with the tan leather reins. They made a turn at the halfway point where Rusty was waiting and then started back.

Estelle made the turn first, but April caught up again. Both Wildfire and Silver were coming on fast at the gallop, and the six spectators were all cheering. Chester was holding a red flag at the finish line, and both riders crossed at the same instant making the race a tie.

"That settles it. I have to be happy with two girls now," ejaculated Bruce.

"Will the girls be happy with this outcome?" inquired Sam.

"I am satisfied for now," said Estelle.

"Bruce can change off dating Estelle and me," added April.

"Maybe I will date you both at the same time," stated Bruce.

Everybody then laughed at the humor.

Autumn was approaching as were colder days while leaves were falling to the music of "Autumn Leaves" by Roger Williams and his piano; the song was often heard on the radio. Ole, Chester, and Louie were putting up a snow fence near their farmhouse.

They just had dinner, and fat Ole belched loudly; then as he was lifting on a heavy wooden post, he blew rapid-fire, tommy-gun farts.

"What good does this snow fence do?" inquired Louie.

"The wood slats stop the force of the blowing snow, and the drifts form away from the house," explained Chester.

"Then there is less snow to shovel after a storm because it piles up by the snow fence," added Ole.

Chester used a sledgehammer to pound the steel posts into the ground, while Ole unraveled a round bale of fence. Louie was using strips of wire to fasten the snow fence to the posts.

Robins and blackbirds were seen in abundance on the land. The birds would be flying south soon, and a flock of geese were then in the sky honking away.

"How do the birds know to fly south?" asked the younger Louie.

"They fly south in late autumn because the sun is in the southern sky at that time, and the birds are merely flying towards the warmth of the sun," explained Chester.

Sunday arrived, and it was an Indian summer day at Lake Winona as Chester and Tamra sat on a park bench near the statue of the Indian maiden Winona.

"Are you going to stay on the farm when you finish college, or enter into a new career?" she asked.

"I am still thinking about it. My agriculture instructor in high school said that one can earn more money than he ever dreamed of by farming," Chester explained.

"Then what is your motive for attending college?" asked Tammy.

"Maybe it is to get away and think for a while and have some new experiences in a new setting. I will get a degree and see what is available for jobs."

"Something interesting will come up because new fields of endeavor open every month," stated Tamra.

No swimmers were seen in the water, but some fishermen were trying their luck near the shore. The hardwood trees on the bluffs above Lake Winona had gold, brown, and scarlet leaves. One bluff was named Sugarloaf with its rocky summit. Not a cloud was seen in the clear sky on that superb day.

Sometime later, Lucy and Ole Borseth were having a big barbecue on their farm in celebration of a wedding anniversary. A substantial crowd was on hand on a mild autumn day with some flowers still in bloom, and squirrels were gathering acorns from oak trees for the long, cold winter ahead.

A whole pig was being roasted outdoors.

"After another twenty-five years, we will be back here for another banquet," said Lester.

Summer Mirage

"With God's blessing, we will all be in attendance for that foggy, unseen day," said Lucy.

"By that time, we will have grandchildren running around," added Ole.

Guests arrived including Bernie and Agnes in their green Studebaker. Then Rusty came in his new 1956 Pontiac; it was a rust color. He brought passengers Sam, Molly, April, Estelle, and Bruce. They piled out of the car, one by one.

"You folks picked the warmest day of the autumn for this barbecue get-together," said Rusty.

"We were just lucky," said Chester.

Lucy and Alice were carving up the roast pig, while others were eating and drinking. The four girls were serving drinks.

Dale Brown approached while Bernie was talking to Lester.

"I did not think you would show up here since Les fired you once," stated Dale.

"Your spooky face is not wanted on this farm," expostulated Bernie.

"I am hungry, and this is where the free food is provided," replied Dale.

"You God damn free loader, I will show you something!" Bernie shouted.

Bernie swung a hard fist to Dale's face, and Dale nearly fell down, but recovered and rushed Bernie, and both toppled to the ground. Each was taking punches before Chester and Rusty came to break up the fight.

"You bad better hit the road, Dale," suggested Chester.

"Do not come back here again!" ordered Bernie, for once giving someone a command.

Dale grabbed a slice of meat before getting into his car and driving off down the road.

"Some people think they can come to any party and bust in," said Rusty.

A new face was seen as April Christmas introduced her sister, Maye. Maye had brown hair, blue eyes, and a slim figure. She was five feet, seven inches tall. Sam was standing with them and looking Maye over.

"Meet my younger sister, Maye!" said April.

"Howdy. You don't seem to resemble your sister," said Sam.

"They say I look like actress Debra Paget in Elvis Presley's first movie, Love Me Tender," said Maye.

"That was a great western movie this year," replied Sam. "They say I resemble Sterling Hayden in the 1950 movie, Asphalt Jungle."

Sam and Maye walked together along a fence with a few cattle and horses grazing nearby in a green pasture.

"What is your character like?" she asked.

"You surprise me by wanting to get personal so quick," Sam noted.

"I want to know as much as possible about a person before I go out on a date. I don't want to be sorry later," said Maye.

"Well, I am known as a sleeper because I lay back and don't show my true intelligence. I pretend to be a novice. Describe your character," requested Sam.

"Amazing! I am less of a flirt than my sister, April. I am more practical and have good ideas, like your brother Rusty," said Maye.

By a coincidence, Bruce and April were having the same conversation while sitting under a Norway pine tree at the big barbecue.

"Describe your character to me," asked Bruce.

"I have been accused of being two-faced because sometimes I flirt with boys, while at other times I am motivated to sit in a library studying for hours. What about you?" she asked.

"I am sometimes a ladies' man because I like to dress up a lot and put on a good appearance. But I am misunderstood. I do not want to appear as a dumb farmer all the time -- with dirt on my clothes and cattle manure on my boots," wisely explained Bruce.

After April left for a while, Estelle joined Bruce.

She sat down by her pal under the pine tree.

"Tell me more about yourself," said Bruce.

"Although I am a brunette, I have just as much fun as the blonde girls. My folks named me after a heroine in the western novel, The Lost Wagon Train, by Zane Grey," explained Estelle.

Summer Mirage

"That is interesting and I like it," replied Bruce.

Rusty and Molly overheard them talking.

"Well, Rusty, it's your turn; tell me about yourself," Molly requested.

"I usually come up with the best ideas. I could be an inventor and get rich that way. Most important of all, I always control my variable temper," stated Rusty.

"Well, friends, besides being called the best cook in the bunch, I avoid anger and try to enhance the quality of each day," said Molly.

"That is smart; just live one day at a time!" said April.

Tamra and Chester came walking and overheard the fine group conversation.

"Well, Chester, what are you like, and what makes you tick?" queried Estelle.

"Well, I also live one day at a time. I am well read and am known to be more mature than my years. Maybe it's because I had some growing up pains, but I did survive and here I am," said Chester.

They reflected on his words.

"As for myself, I am also well read and equal Molly and April in horseback riding. What you see on the outside of a person is only the tip of the iceberg. Each person has hidden desires, ambitions, and fears," stated Tamra.

"You sound like a psychology professor, but it's good, and I like your words," said Bruce with some humor in his tone.

A couple of weeks later, the group of nine friends took their horses and went on a ride into a wooded area. They were a sight to see in their colorful clothes riding amongst the trees with autumn colors of scarlet, gold, and brown.

They came upon a stream, and the horses stopped to drink.

"This reminds me of our camping trip at my farm a few summers ago," said Rusty.

"There were no girls along then," added Sammy.

A fierce windstorm developed with dark clouds. An increasing hard wind came, toppling some trees.

"Watch out; an oak tree is falling down!" shouted Chester.

Bruce and Sam moved fast as it nearly hit them. The weather had changed, and snowflakes were falling.

"We were dressed for mild times, not for this big drop in temperature!" said Tamra.

"Good heavens, we are many miles from home now. We could freeze to death! Don't forget; this is Minnesota!" exclaimed Maye with concern.

"God is not going to let us die," retorted Chester.

"Providing there is a God," returned Sam.

"This is not the time to sound like an atheist!" said Maye.

They rode for a while, but the wind and snow got worse.

"Halt here; we will stop!" said Rusty, taking control of the situation.

The group of nine youths approached him.

"We all have saddle blankets, and I have a couple of brown rolled canvasses tied to my saddle. Let's get under cover!"

All dismounted to tether their horses to tree limbs. Sam, Rusty, Chester, and Bruce fastened canvasses to tree limbs for a wind break while the girls removed the saddle blankets to put around themselves. Heavy snowflakes were falling.

"My blanket is smelly, but warm," said Molly, making the best of the situation.

"Let's get cozy and comfortable!" added April.

"This is just like the Armistice Day storm of November 11, 1940, when duck hunters died from a sudden blizzard along the Mississippi River," said Chester.

"Yeah, the ducks came, and the men died," added Sammy.

"This is an adventure!" put in Estelle.

The blowing snow and fierce wind continued for a long time. An owl sat on a tree branch, blinking his big, golden eyes. A timber wolf lurked behind some bushes and scared off a flock of quail.

After a couple of hours, the storm subsided, and the nine riders took down their shelter and got set to return home. They stopped at the Wampuch farm first. Rusty's little sister, Cindy, a cute blonde preteen girl, was in the yard waiting.

"We were all worried about you people during the blizzard," said Cindy. She wore a fur coat.

"We are tough cowboys and cowgirls," replied Sam.

His parents, Tim and Hilda, emerged from the house. Tim had only one eye, the result of an accident earlier.

"Hilda, you were not worried about us, were you?" asked Rusty, while taking off his black scarf.

"Only a little bit," she replied.

"I knew that my sons could take care of themselves," added Tim. He wore a green flannel shirt and a blue bibbed overall.

"Come in and warm up by the fireplace everybody," Hilda said.

All the robust teenagers gathered around a big and cozy fireplace in a happy mood.

"There is no place like home!" said Estelle, which hinted that she must have seen the movie The Wizard of Oz.

They all took off their coats and caps and rubbed their hands and feet. Hilda brought in cups of hot chocolate.

Cassandra, still a pre-teen, was in the front yard of her home building a snowman. Agnes came walking with a pail of eggs from the chicken coop.

"You are a little old for building a snowman," she said.

"I want to stay as a little girl. Look what happened to Bernie's other girlfriend, Sally."

"I know, she died in a car accident, and an earlier lady named Marigold broke up with Bernie," said Agnes.

"I don't want all those problems of older girls," said her daughter.

Bernie came walking and overheard them. "Just enjoy yourself, Cassandra, while you are young and build another snowman," he suggested.

After sunset, the trio sat on a davenport in front of the cozy fireplace.

"Tell me about yourself, Agnes; what were you doing prior to your marriage to Cliff Jones?"

"I was with the Women's Air Corps, the WAC'S, stationed near Munich, Germany, for a year."

"What? You were in uniform?" ejaculated Bernie.

"That's right. There is more to me than meets the eye. I know all about beer halls on military bases. I even received a scholarship and studied at St. Cloud State College for a year!" proudly stated Agnes.

"Why didn't you stay longer?" asked Cassandra.

"I guess I missed the country life too much. Besides, a couple of the professors were paying too much attention to me."

"Ha, ha, ha, and you had a chance to grab a smart professor who works in an ivory tower," said Bernie.

"Sometimes those ivory towers can get quite boring," replied his wife.

"I am glad you continued with the farm life," said Bernie.

Chapter Twenty

Dale Brown entered a hardware store in Harmony and asked to see the guns. He bought some shells and a Remington bolt-action rifle.

"Are you going squirrel hunting?" asked the male clerk.

Dale grinned with that shit-eating smirk on his face and answered, "Yep, and maybe bigger animals too," leaving it open to conjecture.

Dale sauntered into a tavern and sat at the bar. A pretty brown-haired lady, Lev, wearing a Norwegian style square dance dress, was the bartender.

"What will you have, farm boy?" she asked.

"I will have a shot of Sunnybrook whiskey," Dale responded.

On the walls were mounted heads of deer, wolf, fox, and stuffed ducks. On the Seeberg jukebox, the Kalen Twins were singing their hit song, "When." Dale moved to a corner for more privacy. He was in a pondering mood and spoke in a soliloquy.

"The last trick I played on Bernie was to loosen the nuts on his car wheel, and he drove into a ditch. Then I cut a rope, and a blower pipe fell on him. Bernie has more lives than a tomcat, and I could not scare him to death with monster masks. I owe it to my murdered brother, Steve, to take more drastic action. From now on, it's Bernie or me! No more long delay! One of us is going to Boothill to decay in the ground and return to dust!"

Lev approached in her classy red and white dress. "How about another drink?"

"Yeah, haul over a cold bottle of Grain Belt beer," said Dale. "I like your costume."

The following day, Bernie was out walking in the snow-covered woods hunting for rabbits. He sat on a log and had a cup of hot coffee from a thermos jug. Suddenly, a large cottontail rabbit was jumping around nearby. Bernie sighted his gun and blasted away. "We will have rabbit on the table soon!" he said.

Unknown to him, Dale was also out hunting and heard the shot. He came to check it out and espied Bernie.

"This is too good to be true! That is the bastard that I am after now!" surmised Dale.

He sighted his rifle at Bernie and put a squeeze on the trigger from behind a tree. The latter threw up his hands at the flash and fell backwards on the snow.

"That is one less hired man for the dirt farmers to feed!" stated Dale. He then continued hunting other game.

A few hundred yards away at the Agnes Jones' house, Agnes was getting worried over Bernie's being late for supper. The sun was setting in the gold and purple horizon when the clouds took on colors. The distant forest lay in mystery with its secrets.

"Cassandra, run over by the woods to see if Bernie is on his way home. Maybe he had an accident," suggested Agnes.

"Don't worry, I will find him, Mother," Cassandra said.

As the girl strolled down the driveway, Bernie came walking carrying a rabbit.

"I know I am late for supper, but I bagged some wild meat," he said proudly.

"I was worrying about you, Bernie," said Cassandra.

All entered the wood-frame house together as Agnes opened the door, and they smelled food cooking.

"Look at the dent in my steel belt buckle. Someone took a shot at me, or it was a stray bullet," he said.

"For heavens sake! It's getting dangerous to go hunting now. Well, I will clean the rabbit and put it in the freezer."

Summer Mirage

The trio sat down to a traditional meal of beef, potatoes, squash, and pumpkin pie with whipped cream. Later, they went to the living room to watch Alfred Hitchcock and comedian Milton Berle on their Philco TV set.

The following day, Dale was sitting in a lonely corner in the Niggle restaurant in Rushford eating apple pie and drinking coffee. He glanced out the window to see the white washed sign of RUSHFORD on the wooded bluff. Then Bernie came walking by, and Dale's eyes almost popped out when he became startled.
"I cannot believe it! I bored that bastard, and there he is walking down the sidewalk! What is going on here? I am sure the sights on my gun are right!" ejaculated Dale.
He walked outside the door and stared at Bernie walking.
He talked in a monologue. "Son-of-a-bitch! My job is not done yet. My brother, Steve, will not rest until Bernie Baker is in Boothill pushing up daisies and dandelions!"

It was a Sunday afternoon in Rushford when the brothers, Sam and Rusty, with their girlfriends, Maye and Molly, entered the Trojan Theater. They had warm winter coats on as it was snowing heavily. On the projecting marquee were the letters, Giant, starring James Dean and Elizabeth Taylor.
"Dean was killed in a car accident on September 30, 1955, but he is more popular than ever," stated Maye.
"I like to see Liz Taylor, the brunette," said Rusty.
"I like the blonde one, Carol Baker," replied Sam.
"I like the story of the Texas oilmen and cattlemen," put in Molly.
The theater was about half full of people.

Meanwhile, two other couples, Chester and Tammy, along with Bruce and April, entered the bowling alley in Lewiston.
"Wait until you see a purple ball roll down the lane!" said Chester.
"I have a pink ball and have beaten Bruce a few times," said April.
On the jukebox was playing the tune of "Born Too Late" by the Ponytails.

As they started bowling, the jukebox played "Maybe Baby" by Buddy Holly.

"Can you pick up that split, April?" asked Bruce.

"Don't keep your fingers crossed," she replied.

April heaved her hooking ball and converted the split.

"Good going, April!" exclaimed Tamra.

"We are having fun tonight!" said Bruce.

"That is what we are living for, to have as much fun as possible," stated Tamra with a smile.

A couple of days later, Bruce had already taken his snow tires off his car. As he drove on a gravel road near his big farm, he got stuck from the late season snowfall. He was out shoveling to free his car when Estelle Gill, the gorgeous, slim farm neighbor, stopped to say hello.

"I see you drove too close to the ditch!" she said.

"This is a surprise to see you on a bicycle with snow on the ground yet," returned Bruce.

"You need a bike," suggested the brunette.

"There is a party coming up soon at Rusty's place," Bruce said.

"If you are inviting me, I will gladly go with you," solicited Estelle. She was wearing a brown winter fur coat.

Meanwhile, Ben and Anna Baker arrived at the Jones' farm as their son, Bernie, was shoveling snow from the sidewalk.

"I heard that someone accidentally shot you in the woods, and a steel belt buckle saved you," said Anna.

"News travels fast," replied her son.

"We were on bad terms, but you are still my son," said Ben. "Maybe Dale is out to avenge the demise of his brother Steve."

"I don't doubt that," replied Bernie with a laugh. Dale went to jail for a while for cutting the rope on a blower pipe which fell on me."

"Watch out for any monkey business because tragedies can be prevented," his mother advised wisely.

They entered the house, and Agnes served a tray of cookies with hot chocolate. It was a typical farm kitchen.

"Greetings! I don't get to see you folks often," said Agnes.

Summer Mirage

"What is this about Bernie joining the Alcoholics Anonymous?" asked Anna.

"That's right; I have not taken an alcoholic drink for many months," proudly stated Bernie.

"Amazing! And I had thought you were a no good drunk of a son," returned Ben.

"I am a new man now, no more booze."

After his parents left, Bernie went to the barn and moved chopped hay with a large fork while the radio was playing "The Beer Barrel Polka" by the Six Fat Dutchmen. He then sat down on a sack of feed and talked in a soliloquy. Only the cattle heard him.

"Should Agnes and I have children? Maybe having Cassandra around is enough, but then she is not my real daughter. Maybe we should have a son too."

He rose to clean out the drinking cups of the cows. The cats were drinking milk from a pan.

Some miles away, Dale was loading his rifle with bullets. A bottle of blackberry wine sat on the table next to him.

I have to take a few drinks of wine before I send a man to kingdom come, he said to himself. He lit a cigar and smoked.

On the radio, the Christy Minstrels were singing, "The Ballad of Tom Dooley" as the words, Hang down your head, for tomorrow you will die, were heard. Dale talked in a monologue.

"What if I fail this time? I might end up in jail again. I better not drink too much wine because my reaction time will be slower. Would my late brother approve of my avenging him? Does it make any difference? Well, it does to me, and my mind is set. Both Steve and I will be able to rest after that bastard is sent to Boothill."

He put out his cigar and put on his winter boots, a warm coat, fur cap, scarf, and fur-lined gloves. He knew how to keep warm in the north land; he was not like those stupid city slickers who walked bare headed in thin leather jackets down the sidewalks when it was minus twenty degrees Fahrenheit, and then freeze to death when their cars stalled while out in the boondocks someplace. Dale went out to his blue 1954 Dodge pickup truck and was soon on the road. The wine had caused a lapse of memory, and Dale drove towards the Lester Grey farm instead.

It seemed that he was changeable in his habits; the wine was making him sleepy, and he might put off a confrontation with Bernie for a few days. Nothing was certain except taxes, death, and the rotation of the earth.

Meanwhile, at the Grey farm, Les was pulling on a calf with a rope while Alice was pushing it. They were outside the red barn. They both wore blue Levis trousers.

"I am taking this calf to the sales barn," said Les.

"I will ride along and do some shopping," replied Alice.

They worked together to get the Holstein calf into back of his green 1954 Dodge truck. Les then closed the gate with the calf standing on straw in the rear of thepickup.

"Calf meat is called veal on the table," said Les.

Alice turned on the truck radio and heard "Come Go With Me" by the Del Vikings; then Linda Scott sang "I've Told Every Little Star."

"This is the great music of the Fabulous Fifties!" said the farm wife.

"I wonder how the Soaring Sixties will be?" asked Les.

"Only God knows," she returned.

They drove towards Lewiston.

After they had returned home, Dale Brown, average looking with brown hair, drove into the farm yard of the Grey's.

"Are you lost or are you selling something?" queried Lester.

"I heard that Bernie Baker is here, and I'd like to talk to him," said Dale.

"He is a hired man for Agnes Jones down by Harmony; they got married some time ago," replied Les.

Dale tipped his Stetson hat and then took leave in his truck with Les standing and watching dust from the vehicle.

I know where Bernie is, but I just want to meet his former boss, said Dale to himself.

Summer Mirage

On a farm near Harmony, in Fillmore County, Minnesota, Bernie parked the Allis Chalmars tractor next to the red gas barrel. He was putting in gas when Agnes approached.

"Can you sweep down the cobwebs in the barn today, Bernie?"

"Yeah, it's a good idea to clean that place up," Bernie agreed.

"That deer meat you got is good," she commented.

"It is healthy food," said Bernie.

After the noon lunch, he picked up a broom and swept down the spider webs from the walls and ceiling in the red barn.

"I will fix them damn ugly spiders!" he said.

Bernie turned on the RCA barn radio and listened to a few songs, "Have You Heard" and "Why Don't You Believe Me" by Joni James. He espied mice crawling along the walls and running into holes. Agnes came to assist and grabbed a broom to sweep down more spider webs. She also noticed the mice running around.

"We need more cats here; that's why we see so many mice," said Agnes.

"I know where we can get more cats," said Bernie. "Les Grey has more than he needs. We need more here to get rid of the mice that are messing around in the oats and corn."

"You can drive over to Les' farm on Sunday and ask him for a few cats," she suggested.

They finished their task in time for supper. Agnes was a good mate because she was willing to do the same work as Bernie. Later, they milked the forty cows in the barn and fed them hay. After chores, they walked back to the house, which was only a long stone's throw from the barn. The brown-haired Cassandra was putting a puzzle together.

"What are you making?" asked Bernie.

"It's going to be a church. Do you like puzzles?" asked the girl in a yellow dress.

"No, they are too hard for me to figure out, and I do not have much patience."

"What shall we have for Thanksgiving dinner?" he asked while turning towards Agnes.

"Turkey and many goodies," replied his wife, the fair-haired lady who was still attractive.

"Do you like turkey?" she asked him.

"Oh, hell, yes, but it don't like me," replied Bernie.

"Ha, ha, ha," uttered mother and daughter.

"I like you, Bernie," said Cassandra.

The trio then looked at "Bonanza" on the black and white TV screen.

"I'd like to own a ranch like the Cartwright's ranch," said Bernie.

"That countryside would look good in color," replied Agnes.

The family retired to bed after the local news. Snow was falling, at first in small grain-like flakes, as winter was setting in. Cassandra was happy in her own bedroom.

The following Sunday, Bernie drove into the yard of his one-time boss, Les Grey. He stepped out of his brown 1952 Nash car as Lester came walking.

"Look who is in Winona County again," said Les. "Come into the house; you are just in time for lunch."

"Thanks, I'm as hungry as a wolf when the deer and rabbit populations are down," stated Bernie.

Alice was in the kitchen cutting up a few pieces of cake and brewing coffee. "Hi, Bernie," she greeted him while smiling.

"Hello, Alice, I see you are as busy as usual," Bernie responded.

The men seated themselves at the table, and Alice brought on carrot cake and coffee.

"Do you still have a lot of cats around here?" asked Bernie.

"I got more damn cats than I want," replied Les.

"Sometimes I put kittens in a plastic bag to suffocate them."

"Agnes and I want a few extra cats to help control the mice on our farm. We don't have enough cats, and the barn and granary are crawling with mice. We have a dog who gets rid of the rats," explained Bernie.

The men finished eating lunch, then stalked out to the red, wood-frame barn.

"Here are two young yellow cats and a gray one that are *good* mice killers," said Les.

They picked up the cats.

Summer Mirage

"There is a sack in the feed room that you can carry the cats in," said Les.

"Cats have put mice in their diet for thousands of years," added Bernie, who sometimes seemed wise in spite of being profane and having been a heavy drinker of alcoholic beverages.

Bernie then drove back towards Harmony, asking himself how that town got its name. As he emerged from his brown Nash car, Cassandra was outside playing with a collie pup. White, fluffy, cumulus clouds dotted the sky.

"Guess what I got in this sack?" he asked.

"Something is moving in there!" she replied.

Bernie moved closer and yanked out a yellow cat.

"Oh, boy, he is cute!" said Cassandra.

"It's for you!" Bernie took out the other two cats and placed them by the girl.

"They are all so cute!" she said. It was the happiest that she had been all month. She took one into the house.

"Look, Mommy, what Bernie gave me!"

Later, the cats were in the barn and doing their duty, like all good cats should, catching mice and eating them as fast as they could. They had a real banquet!

Chapter Twenty-One

It was Thanksgiving Eve at the Wampuch farm as Chester and his girl drove into the yard and parked near the trees.

"It is cold out," said Tamra as she was shivering.

Rusty greeted them at the door. "Welcome to the party!"

They marched in and espied Molly Olson pouring Seven-Up into glasses. "Hi, Chester and Tamra," she said.

"Howdy! How are you doing?" he replied.

"Great, want any ice in your drinks?" asked Molly, the cute, lovely, slim girl with brown hair and hazel eyes.

"I never take ice during the cold season because I almost froze up riding my bicycle a mile and a half to a country school in my younger days," stated Chester.

The room was decorated with holiday things and was bright with colors. Bruce Thompson entered the room with his gorgeous brunette, Estelle Gill, who could be a sweater girl on the cover of Movie Life magazine.

"Hello, friends!" they greeted everyone.

"Bruce keeps telling me about that great and memorable summer vacation you guys had while going camping and horseback riding some time ago," said Estelle. "You farmers are unique."

"That was a fun time," replied Chester.

"What is on the agenda tonight?" asked Tamra, the auburn-haired, hazel-eyed beauty.

"Anything we can think of that's fun!" answered Molly, as Rusty winked at Chester during that open-ended suggestion.

"Where are you from, Estelle?" he asked.

"From the sleepy hamlet of Peterson, a nice town nestled between the bluffs and a creek, but I live on a farm now," said Estelle. She wore a green sweater and brown slacks.

"Interesting, one of my grandparents is from there too," said Chester. "I have noticed that the Germans settled on more level land and drilled wells for water, while the Norwegians settled along the creeks and rivers where water was available."

They all got comfortable on a davenport and watched an episode of "Alfred Hitchcock," a mystery.

"It always has an unexpected ending," said Bruce.

"Where is Sam tonight?" asked Molly.

"He went out with Maye bowling," said Rusty.

After the TV show was over, Estelle and Bruce stood Molly and Rusty in a game of "500" at cards. Tamra and Chester sat down to a game of chess on the onyx stone set from Mexico. He had been trying to improve his abilities at chess since Tamra was an expert. Chester moved all his pieces off the back row except the rooks and king and then castled.

He set up a good defense while she was advancing with a knight and queen. She could not find an opening. Soon, both players had lost a few pawns and a bishop. He placed his queen in front of his rook and had a bishop in a corner. Chester then sacrificed a knight and moved the queen down for the checkmate.

"You pulled a fast one on me!" said Tamra.

"It was my turn to win anyway," he replied with a smile.

On the Decca phonograph was heard Gene Autry singing, "Up on the House-Top" and "Here Comes Santa Claus."

"Who is winning the card game?" asked Chester.

"Bruce and I won the first game," announced Estelle.

"Everyone for more drinks, give us a Comanche war cry!" said Bruce.

The girls had never heard it, so Rusty and Chester yelled, "Kanee-Wah!" and all laughed.

"My goodness, where did you come up with that?" asked Molly.

"From the Straight Arrow comic books and his radio program," replied Chester.

The boys entered the kitchen to pour mixed drinks of Seven-Up and Scotch whiskey.

"We are pudner adults, so we may as well drink like adults," said the intelligent Rusty.

They were all having a splendid party at his farm while his folks were absent. Soon, the girls put on more phonograph records, and all hugged and danced to the "Tennessee Waltz" sung by the fair-haired Patty Page, the singing rage.

Tamra turned down the lights, and the scene became romantic while the snow was falling outside. They listened to the world's best-selling song, "White Christmas," by Bing Crosby with his clear and soothing voice; it was playing on the radio. The German shepherd, Pluto, was peeking in the bay window, wondering what all the noise and music was about.

"You did great in football this autumn," said Chester.

"I was lucky to make All-Conference," replied Rusty.

"Are you going out for basketball?" asked Estelle.

"No, I don't like to run up and down a hardwood floor and jump up and down like a jackrabbit or a kangaroo," explained the athlete, Rusty.

"Ha, ha, ha," all laughed in unison.

"Hey, we are having a good time!" said Chester.

Then they all danced to "The Summer Place" by Percy Faith. Later, they sat down to a lunch prepared by the three girls.

"The ornate tablecloth was made by my grandmother," proudly stated Molly.

"What are you majoring in at college?" asked Tamra.

"I don't know yet because new careers may be created while I am still in college," said Rusty's favorite girl.

"The rye bread sandwiches with deer meat, lettuce, apple sauce, sunflower seeds, and milk are great for a meal," announced Chester.

"Thanks, junk food is not good enough for a superb group like us," replied Molly.

After the lunch, they returned to the Philco television set to watch a late movie. On the boob tube was "The Wolf Man" with Lon Cheney, Jr. and Evelyn Ankers; it was a horror film.

"How would you like to meet him out on the doorsteps?" asked Chester.

"Do not scare me so!" replied Tammy.

They stayed until the movie was over; then the farewells were said as Molly and Rusty remained at home. They were all in the holiday spirit.

As Chester drove Tamra home, the yard light was on in the driveway, and the light sparkled off her diamond ring.

"Many thanks for a memorable evening," she said.

"We are both quite thankful for good friends and parents," he replied.

They then shared a warm goodnight kiss while still in his car.

Tamra Hunt strolled up the path to her house while her pal left in his blue Chevy to return home. The snow was still falling, and the clouds covered the full moon most of the night.

A humorous thought occurred to Chester, The Wolf Man will have a hard time seeing the full moon tonight!

Chapter Twenty-Two

As the sun raised its pretty head in the eastern horizon, there was a pink glow, and the gray clouds were lined in silver. The countryside was pure with white snow, including the tall trees. There were sloping hills to the east of the Jones' farm near Harmony, then occupied by Agnes and Bernie Baker.

To the south were woods. The fields had been harvested of corn and hay. Only the hazel-colored stubble remained.

It was Thanksgiving morning as Bernie stalked up to the barn to milk the cows. Bernie saw Agnes pouring milk into a pan for the cats, and he reached down to pet them.

"Good morning, are we all going to the church dinner today?" she asked.

"Happy holidays! Yep, they always serve good food in a church."

The two farmers milked the cows, fed them corn silage and ground oats and corn, and washed the milking utensils. Back at the house, Cassandra was the first to get her best clothes on.

"What kind of puzzle are you making?" asked the nosy Bernie.

"It is to be some boys swimming in a pond."

"It looks good," Bernie replied.

She smiled at Bernie.

Soon, the family was off to church, and they sat together on the pine wood seats. The preacher was talking about the history of the Roman Empire and the part that the early Christians played in it.

Summer Mirage

After the sermon, there was a line of people waiting to be served a dinner. Bernie stood in line behind Agnes, Cassandra, and a nun, dressed in black.

"Son-of-a-bitch, what are they holding us up for?" uttered Bernie, loud enough for everybody to hear.

Everyone laughed at his rudeness. Shortly after, the old minister walked by the line of hungry people; he did not hear Bernie. Finally, the Ladies Aid began serving the meal, and everyone took seats at the long table. It was the familiar Thanksgiving dinner with turkey, corn, potatoes, cranberries, buns, pumpkin pie with whipped cream, and milk.

Afterwards, Agnes, Cassandra, and Bernie piled into the green 1954 Studebaker and headed for home.

"If I had eaten more, I would be as bloated as a steer grazing in a new field of alfalfa!" stated Bernie.

"Me too!" said Cassandra, while wearing a yellow dress.

That afternoon, the family relaxed in the living room and watched a college football game on TV. Agnes carried in bottles of grape soda pop.

"That really hits the spot!" said Bernie.

Soon after, Bernie thought he wanted more to drink. What the hell; it's a holiday, he said to himself.

He walked to the feed room near the barn and snatched a bottle of blackberry wine from behind some fifty pound RCC mineral sacks. He sat down on the sacks to drink.

"I will not get drunk because I am now just a social drinker," he rationalized.

Later, Bernie was cleaning out a calf pen with a four-tine pitchfork and heaving the manure into a spreader. He did not see an intruder enter the sliding barn door. Dale Brown approached holding a .22 rifle.

"Well, look who is working. You killed my brother Steve many months ago up in a hay loft, and I never believed your story in court," stated Dale. He looked menacing and evil.

"You God damn dumb shit! Steve was not worth the powder to blow a fucker to hell, and he was monkeying around with my girlfriend, Marigold Clausen!" replied Bernie.

"You are the strangest, 'drunkenest' hired man I ever saw, and I am sending you on a one-way vacation trip to Boothill!"

Bernie made a sudden half-turn and heaved the sharp pitchfork into the chest of Dale, who in turn fired his gun at the same moment. Bernie was hit, and both men slumped down in agony and uttered cries of pain. The calves were frightened nearby.

Meanwhile, back at the house, Agnes watched a football player kick a field goal to win the game.

"What a game, but I will be glad when the last foolish game is played this season," she said.

"I like the pass plays best," commented Cassandra, who was soon to be a teenager.

Around six in the evening, Agnes set the table and made supper. "Cassandra, please go up to the barn and tell Bernie that supper is ready," said Agnes.

"All right, Mother," replied the pretty daughter.

Agnes may have resembled her some twenty-five years earlier.

Cassandra put on a blue scarf, brown mackinaw coat, a warm green cap, and winter boots and walked out to the barn. She put her hands in the coat pockets to keep them warm.

The girl noticed that the barn door was open, and she entered. The cows standing in stanchions looked at her.

"Supper is ready, Bernie!" she shouted.

The cows mooed, and the calves bawled, and she almost stumbled over a yellow cat.

"I wonder where Bernie is?" she said. She looked in the feed room and espied an empty wine bottle.

Then Cassandra walked down the aisle between the calf pens and stanchions. In the second pen, she saw a body lying in the manure and filth. Cassandra screamed when she knew it was Bernie.

"My friend, Bernie, what happened?"

Then she came upon the body of Dale with a pitchfork stuck in his chest as he lay on his back. The farmer's daughter ran to the house.

"What is it?" asked Agnes in concern.

"Call the ambulance and the sheriff! Bernie and another man are lying in the barn in bad shape!" cried out Cassandra.

Within a short time, both vehicles arrived to do their work. Bernie was washed off with a water hose in the milk house.

"He is as dead as a dusty mummy in a pyramid," said the medical man.

"So is Dale Brown," said the fat sheriff, George.

"Oh, heavens, now I have to waste another five hundred dollars on a tear-jerking funeral to bury my second husband," said Agnes.

"I did not think you would be worried about your bank account now," said the ambulance driver.

"Maybe I will cry tomorrow because I have a slow reaction time," replied Agnes.

There was a lot of excitement in the two-story, white painted frame house, built in the lumber of the 1880's. Bernie Baker's journey on planet Earth was at an end, and Cassandra was crying.

A mild spell spread across the upper Midwest, bringing warmer temperatures. A black hearse pulled up to the Catholic Church in Harmony, where Bernie had some times frequented. Ben and Anna Baker were among the people watching.

Six people then carried out the charcoal gray casket that contained the body of Bernie. Les Grey, Louie and Chester Borseth, Rusty and Sam Wampuch, and Bruce Thompson were all in their Sunday best suits. The church bells commenced ringing.

They carried the cold, dead meat, which had once been Bernie, into the church where he lay for an hour, as the old man in a black robe spoke. Then the pallbearers took the casket back to the hearse. Soon, Bernie was taking his last ride ever on the good Earth. The funeral procession proceeded with the headlights on all of the cars and pickup trucks.

Most of the snow had melted, and it was cloudy out, for rain was threatening. The procession pulled up to the Memorial Park, and the people exited their vehicles. The six pallbearers carried the dead hired man to a hole in the ground.

The dirt on top was of a black, sandy loam. A redheaded woodpecker was busy on a tree nearby, probably looking for ants.

The people crowded around the preacher as he read from a black book; then he crossed himself as if doing some kind of magic. Anna, the mother, was wiping tears from her eyes, while Ben, her husband, was reticent and sober. The honey blonde lady and one-time girlfriend of Bernie, Marigold Clausen, was with the mourners in attendance. She wore a pink hat and a green coat.

All the girlfriends, including both of Bruce's women, of the pallbearers were in attendance wearing colorful clothes. The crowd was small in numbers.

The people then filed back to their cars to return to the church to eat a lunch, and the older persons would add to their middle-aged bulges.

Some time later, two men went to where the deadman had been lowered into a shallow hole. They shoveled dirt on top of the casket and vault. A while later, the graveyard was deserted except for woodpeckers.

Then a badger walked across the church grounds. Suddenly, lightning streaked across the sky, followed by thunder. As the day drew to a close, the rain began to fall, melting the last patches of snow and erasing all the footprints. Bernie was resting in peace, and life went on for everyone else.